STRUGGLING

FOR LOVE
AND LIFE

"BY LINDA FOSTER"

BLOSSOM PUBLISHING HOUSE

BLOSSOM PUBLISHING HOUSE
P.O. Box 4
Mckeesport, Pa.15134

Manufactured in the United States of America

Struggling for Love and Life

ISBN-13: 978-0615816708
ISBN-10: 0615816703

Printed in the United States of America

Library of Congress Control Number: 2013907601

"For Battered Women and Survivors"

ACKNOWLEDGMENTS

Heavenly Father, I am so grateful for your protection and patience. Thank you for allowing me to share my story. The honor, glory, and praise belong solely to you.

Dad, thank you for your financial support and praying for me through my storms. Thank you for being my number one Bishop, Pastor, and Father. I love you.

Mom, after 25 years, I finally finished. I will see you when I get there, and then we will celebrate. Thank you for the memories that will never fade.

Aurelia, I bet you are up there with mom laughing away. Thanks for rejoicing for me.

Juakina, Mylisha, and Leon, I truly thank you for believing in me and not judging me because of my past. I just want to encourage you to follow your dreams. Never let anyone tell you that you can't. Set goals. Be an unseen giver. Stay humble. Believe in yourself no matter what happens in your life. Most of all put God first in everything you do. I love you all unconditionally. Leon, never say you can't. You can and you will.

Elizabeth, you are a precious sibling. Thank you for being a big part of my life, and this story. I wouldn't trade you in for nothing in the world.

Paul, thank you for your genuine concern and doing whatever you could.

Jacalyn, you are my very best friend. Thank you for your encouragement and believing in me, even before you read my story. You prayed for my family and me. In spite of your obligations at home, you sacrificed your time. You've offered your expertise in areas that I had no knowledge. I can't thank you enough and don't know what I would have done without you.

Erin, I thank you for sacrificing your time by helping me with your knowledge in editing. I appreciate you.

Janet, you were God Sent. You came to my rescue at the right time. Thank you for tremendously fixing some of the errors on the manuscript. I didn't know where to begin.

The Pratt Family, you have been an inspiration to me. Thank you for your prayers.

Joann, you were a ram in the bush when it was time to make changes in my book. May God richly bless you for your labor of love.

Introduction

Struggling For Love And Life is a fiction based on a true story about the price paid by being in the wrong relationship. Mentally and physically abused victims don't always realize that there is help. For some, it is a way of life to survive. For others, it may seem that there is just no way out. Yet, other's wait to late for help.

I am a survivor. What I went through may seem shocking and unreal. The mental and physical abuse actually happened. This book will enlighten battered victims of a better life filled with unconditional love and forgiveness.

The wrong perception of love led me on a destructive journey. I should have taken heed to the warning signs sooner. I struggled for his love, and eventually struggled for my life. The story ends in tragedy.

CHAPTER ONE

THE WORST YEARS OF MY LIFE began on June 30, 1978. The weather appeared to be extremely seasonable. As I glanced up, there was an arc of colors formed by the refraction and reflection of the sun's rays. What a beautiful sight to see! While gazing at the sky, a red robin flew passed me chirping away. For a moment, my thoughts were again about meeting a gallant knight taking me off into the sunset. Reality quickly set in as I began to take a walk.

It was about 5 p.m., when I ran into a few acquaintances while walking down the street. We decided to go to the "Riverview Bar." This popular establishment was located in the mid-section of town operating between the hours of 12 p.m. to 2 a.m. A good time was undoubtedly explicit when hanging out in this bar.

When you first walked in, the left side consisted of approximately six or seven antique wooden tables. Each comfortably seated about four people. In between the tables, appeared a flashy new-colorful jukebox, which had the capacity to play generally about fifty different songs by various artists. Additional tables and chairs were located towards the rear near the restrooms.

I admired the whole setup, which included the sparkling dance floor located between the bar and the tables in the back. Just about twenty-five to thirty people could dance comfortably without bumping into each other.

Yes, this was the place to be where a woman could possibly find her "Mr. Right." My friends and I gathered around the pool table trying to decide who would play first.

1

I was a 21-year-old, single parent, living at my parents' home in a small rural town in Denver, Colorado. My father, Reuben Darnell Jones, was the Pastor of "Holiness Church of God in Christ." He succeeded the late Reverend Norman C. Jackson. The church was located on Ninth Street and had roughly 300 members.

My hard-working dad was born and raised in the state of Alabama. He grew up on a farm, which consisted of raising pigs, cows, and chickens. In suitable time, family members slaughtered and sold the animals or butchered them for a meal. They also planted their own fruits, vegetables, and nuts.

At the age of four, I lived with my grandmother, Claudia Mae Mathews Jones. I stayed with her for about a year until it was time for me to start kindergarten.

While being there, I always hoped for the chore of picking fresh pecans. Shaking the trees made it so much easier, while hoping the nuts would not pluck me on my forehead.

Among other duties, I dreaded the task of picking corn while walking through the fields. Thoughts of possibly seeing a snake had me petrified.

Grandmother had a well located in front of the house, which replaced the absence of running water. While fearfully and hesitantly peeking down that bottomless pit, my imagination got the best of me. I thought that crocodiles, alligators, and other fierce creatures were waiting to jump up, snatch me into the dungeon, and swallow me whole.

The outhouse was just as bad as looking down that well. I expected a rat or some other crawling creature would come from the underground and bite me on the buttocks.

While minding and doing my own business in the outhouse, I encountered several attacks. As my half-bent body kept a keen eye on the volcano-like hole, a life-sized bumblebee appeared out of nowhere buzzing as if it owned the place. One of us had to go. I panicked and screamed at the top of my lungs. This horrific episode caused me to jump up instantaneously, practically tripping, while running as fast as possible with my pants down to my knees. Forgetting about those awful days never happened.

A round, rusty-metal basin always hung on the outside wall of the house for easy accessibility for bath time. Grandmother would fill it up with buckets of water from the well. The hot temperatures made the cool bath a pleasant way to refresh. Because of the houses being so far apart, the thought of neighbors seeing you bathe was not a concern.

Quite often, I did not want to go outside due to the unbearable heat and the giant-sized bugs that flew often passed my head. They seemed to be everywhere, including the red ants.

Many times, I walked with my head down, making sure not to invade the military army's territory. Sitting on the benches was no exception. Frequently lifting my feet, kept those horrifying critters from attacking my toes. Why my parents left me in such a place was beyond my imagination.

In spite of the unpleasant moments, grandmother was a good cook, which made my stay somewhat enjoyable. She would let me feast on whatever I wanted. The excitement of playtime was rewarding after my belly became full.

My cousin, Rachel and I, enjoyed taking turns pushing each other on the swing set in the back yard.

We also had a lot of fun venturing through the fields to see Aunt Sheila. The inside of her small house looked like a cluttered barn. Rachel and I would snicker behind her back because Aunt Sheila did not have any teeth, which made her talk funny.

My grandmother had a brother who lived in a trailer behind her house. Uncle Roy made his own whisky. I was so afraid of him and would often run and hide--especially if he was drunk. If he looked at me strange and spoke, I cried and wanted my daddy to come and get me to take me home. Unfortunately, the distance played a big factor for dad not coming to my rescue.

My 50-year-old father dressed neat and was always clean-shaven. He started developing gray hair at the early age of 35. His height was about 5' 11", and he weighed a little over 170 pounds. Although you couldn't tell, most of his clothing came from second-hand stores. Dad faithfully alternated his only two suits when going to church or other special events. In spite of practically living from paycheck to paycheck, he was absolutely a good provider for the family.

In my younger days, I perceived him to be very stern. As I got a little older, a detection of his humorous side surfaced. No matter how many times he told the same story about his childhood days, the comical side never lessened.

One of the stories centered on his brother, Harvey, during their teenage years. Uncle Harvey, the younger of the two, stayed in trouble. One day, he put on my father's shoes, took the family car without permission, and purposely left it in the middle of the street to get dad in trouble. When my grandparents discovered the vehicle, my dad received a beating. His shoe tracks had embedded the red dirt leading up to the vehicle. They did not believe him when he denied committing the mischievous act. Since they recognized his footprints, as far as they were concerned, he was the culprit.

Although Uncle Harvey tried his best to keep his distance, dad would sit back and wait for the right timing to get his revenge. When the opportunity presented itself, dad beat the crap out of him.

My favorite story centered on 11-year-old Rudy, the bully, who was about twice dad's height and weight. Rudy repeatedly picked on dad and on occasion took his school lunch. My father became very upset but refused to do anything because he thought the boy could beat him. After a year of this routine intimidation, my frustrated father went home and decided to tell his mother.

Grandmother pointed her finger and said, "Boy, the next time Rudy picks on you or take your lunch, you better knock his head off! If you don't, when you come home, I'm going to beat you into the middle of next week!"

Dad regretted telling her and now felt pressured to make some quick decisions. He said he would rather lose a fight to Rudy than have his momma beat the crap out of him. Showing mercy was not an option. Grandma would have made him pick his own switch, and it had better not be a thin one.

The next day, Rudy started his usual routine by stealing and eating dad's lunch. It consisted of a peanut butter and jelly sandwich, a pear, a chocolate chip cookie, and a carton of milk. After school, Rudy came out of nowhere and pushed my father into some bushes.

Dad immediately remembered the words of his mother and visualized her beating him with a thick switch. Disobeying his mother remained unthinkable. Reluctantly, and not knowing what the outcome would be, he got up and flexed his muscles. Next, he balled his fists, closed his eyes, and punched Rudy with all his might. Lo and behold, he knocked poor Rudy on the ground. Rudy started crying, got up, and ran into the opposite direction. After realizing the victorious moment he encountered, Dad felt like a champion. He chased after Rudy while still flexing his muscles. He was the man, and you could not tell him anything different.

Fortunately, Rudy being a track star could run as fast as lightening. He made it home without another incident that day and never bullied dad or took his lunch again. The next day, Rudy brought in candy as a peace offering, and they became friends for life. Shortly thereafter, rumors circulated that dad was a famous young boxer in disguise.

When dad got home that day, the excitement showed all over his face. The fact that his mom had company never crossed his mind. He interrupted their conversation and courageously interjected, while leaping for joy, "Ma, I knocked Rudy's head off like you told me to do!"

Grandmother's demeanor drastically changed. Right away, dad noticed the presence of Rudy's mom. It was too late to take those bragging words back. Grandmother was so embarrassed.

She looked harshly in dad's eyes and said, "Boy, you know good and well I didn't tell you to do that. Why you lying on me, Sonny. Go get me a switch!"

Mom and I would laugh every time we heard that story. Whenever my mother would think about something funny, she would cackle like the mannequin at "Sherwood Amusement Park." Her downright hilarious chuckle would make you giggle without even knowing why you were laughing.

My 44-year-old mother, Lydia Lynn Jones, was the oldest of ten children. She was 5' 7" and weighed about 250 pounds. She had the smoothest brown skin tone one could ever imagine. Mother's hair had thinned over the years, so she decided to buy several different wigs to wear for special occasions, including church. Her favorite was the medium length, off-black hairpiece, which she styled and pinned in a cornrow.

Mom always dressed in moderation. Her religious background taught her that a Christian woman should not wear pants. However, wearing culottes seemed to be satisfactory. That was as close as she would get without feeling disobedient to the tradition.

Grandma Smith had instilled good family values in my mom, which made her the perfect helpmate for my father. She was his backbone. Momma paid the bills, kept the house clean, cooked, and took care of our family with what she had. She was very conservative. Powdered milk, surplus meat, and government cheese helped to make our meals stretch, and we were grateful.

Mom worked as a nurse's aide in her early years. In addition, she cleaned and ironed for others to bring in extra money.

She was a meticulous house cleaner and believed spring and fall cleaning should be done every year. This included wiping down the walls, baseboards, and sending curtains to the dry cleaners, which made the creases perfect. When finished, the house sparkled from top to bottom.

If Mom didn't feel like doing the anticipated work, one or two people were hired. That would be either Mrs. Jeannie Wright or Mrs. Evelyn Roberts. Her faithful friends did excellent work.

I had two sisters. Lorraine was six years younger and Marie was a year older than I was. My brother, Mark, was two years apart from me. We were the typical African-American family with a low to modest income.

Because of the ministry we came up under, my dad made us go to church nearly every Sunday, Tuesday, and Friday. In addition to regular services, occasional revivals during the week would last until midnight. Staying home to play with my friends was not an option.

Whenever dad's car broke down, our family faithfully walked about a mile and a half to church. Echoes seemed to follow us while people stared or laughed. Dad carried his Bible in his right hand, and Mom carried her favorite tambourine. She always seemed to have the joy of the Lord, and frequently sang as we walked. This embarrassed me many times, but in spite of our circumstances, we did what we had to do. The time would come someday for me to make my own decisions about going to church, and I couldn't wait.

Not all my decisions were good ones. At the age of 16, I became pregnant by a young man named John Justin. He was an outstanding quarterback for our number one rated high school football team. In his senior year, he received a scholarship to go to a well- known college located in Dallas, Texas.

After the initial shock, concerning my pregnancy, we talked about marriage but concluded that neither one of us was ready for a commitment. He desired to pursue his dream of becoming a professional football player. John made it clear that the opportunity of a lifetime may not come around again. I pretended to understand, not knowing what to say or do when he walked away from me for good. Being 16 and pregnant had never been on my agenda.

During the first five months of pregnancy, morning sickness got the best of me. The doctor diagnosed me as having an iron deficiency. The frequent cramps made me so miserable.

In spite of my adversity, my determination never deterred from raising my daughter, Tina, to the best of my ability. That was a priority in my life. In the beginning, I really was clueless about motherhood.

In spite of hurting my parents, I was grateful they didn't turn their back on me. When they first realized about my pregnancy, they were devastated. My father had preached against such sin. Being an honor roll student in high school had prepared me to be the most likely to succeed out of all the siblings.

Unfortunately, it took a while for me to hold my head up high because of the embarrassment for myself, as well as for my parents. I really let them down.

Adjusting to my predicament took a little time for them, but things got better in due time. This would be there first grandchild and I appreciated their support in helping me raise Tina.

Learning to be a mother encountered a few run-ins with mom. The first week home, mom accidentally dropped my baby. A little past midnight, mom fell asleep on the recliner with Tina lying across her lap. All of a sudden, there was a loud thump. Seconds later, my baby screamed to the top of her lungs.

On impulse, I jumped out of bed and made my way downstairs. The birth had taken a toll on my body so movement was very slow.

Mom was bending over picking Tina up from the floor. When she saw me, she started hollering and made it clear that the doctor's orders stated that I should not be going up and down those steps.

This incident made me very upset. "Mom, you dropped her! I want my baby!"

7

Mom yelled right back. "Who you think you raising your voice at? She's all right. Go back to bed!"

The fussing continued while reluctantly marching back upstairs. I wanted so much to go and grab my baby from my mother, but reluctant in case of drama.

The rest of the night seemed quiet but endless. I didn't sleep very well and attentively listened to make sure there wasn't another episode.

Inquisitive Tina seemed to grow overnight. Before long, she was crawling, walking, and getting into everything possible. It would not have been easy for me to raise her without help.

The necessity of me living with my parents made it convenient; I could come and go as I pleased. Mom would babysit and there was peace, knowing that Tina was safe.

My cute and chubby daughter remained toothless for what seemed forever. When attempting to braid her short hair, my child would throw a fit. Many times, waiting for her to go to sleep in order to finish her hair, was my best option. When she woke up, I told her how pretty she looked. She would smile.

Her wide grin would perk up anyone. When Tina got excited, she jumped up and down wearing that beautiful smile.

She loved to dance, and play with baby dolls while pretending to be their mother. Tina would dress them, and comb their hair. After feeding her dolls, she patted them on the back and made hilarious burping sounds. Finally, she would cuddle up with her babies until all were asleep. The toys and accessories were everywhere.

Originally, my plans consisted of going to college to obtain a nursing degree. Prior to high school graduation, an opportunity presented itself and my life went into a completely different direction. I found a job working on the batteries at the local steel mill. The money was good.

In addition, I worked part-time at "Julia's Ice Cream Store" while in high school. This second full-time job at the mill made it possible for me to dress my daughter with the finest from "Seventh Avenue Clothing Store." I felt very independent.

As my friends and I gathered around the pool table, a couple of fellows entered the bar. My assumption was that they were from out of town. As they glanced in my direction, a sheepish manner immediately surfaced. I quickly turned my head.

I was wearing my "wild wig." Because of my long, unruly hair, wigs were a solution to numerous bad hair days. This particular one was off black, long, and curly. Spraying it with moisturizer made it easier to comb and gave it a nice shine. Afterwards, my fake hair seemed to bounce while walking. This made me feel more outgoing and jovial.

While waiting for a turn at the pool table, the strangers talked to several people who seemed to be acquaintances. Apparently, this was not their first time here. They ordered a shot of something and reminisced at the bar for about half an hour.

I had almost forgotten about them until one of the men tapped me on the shoulder. I turned around to look into the darkest brown eyes that I had ever seen. They seemed to glitter in the glow of the bar's subtle lights. My heart stood still for a moment while wondering what he could possibly have to say to me.

The man's handsome face formed a friendly, crooked smile. "Hey you! What's your name?" All of a sudden, the noise from the jukebox and crowds in the background seemed to fade away.

"Sarah Jones," I said, trying to keep my voice from squeaking, while pushing my glasses up on my nose.

"Name is William Taylor, but call me Bill." He wore a big, brown leather hat that cocked to the side. It looked like a sombrero and set off the darkness of his ebony eyes and rich black skin.

Bill was slender and about a half inch to an inch shorter than me. His beard and mustache made him look a lot older, maybe thirtyish or more. I found out later that he had just turned 23.

"Are you from around here?" I asked while trying to make conversation.

"No, New York. I'm here wit my cous, 'just chillin' for a while." Quickly, he scanned around the pool table, looking at my friends who either had paired off or were standing by themselves.

"Where's yo man?"

I looked around to make sure he was talking to me. "I don't have one."

I had a friend named Bobby Henson. We had known each other since high school. He considered me as his other woman. However, I did not see the relationship in the same way.

While constantly on the lookout for a real man of my dreams, hanging around Bobby was just for male companionship. I longed for a fun, loving, tall and handsome man to sweep me off my feet. Anticipation for a father figure that would love, accept and treat me and my daughter right, was always in the back of my mind. Bobby, however, did not fit these standards.

As I glanced at Bill, he captured my attention. His happy-go-lucky attitude made me inquisitive while observing his actions the rest of the night. His cool interaction with other people astonished me. People would walk up to him, shake his hands, or slap him five. Whatever he did or said seemed to please them.

If I didn't know any better, one would think that Bill was giving out winning lottery tickets. I marveled at how cordial everyone had been towards him. Those that engaged in conversation responded with much laughter. They seemed to be having a heck of a good time.

Because of my not so great self-esteem, I shied away from attempts to have many friends. The feeling of not being street smart or good enough to hang around certain people made me cautious about being too sociable. In addition, my clothes were not as fashionable as my peers were. I didn't wear the name brands.

In my younger years, because of my height, most boys were shorter. Looking down on them gave me an uncomfortable feeling, especially at parties. For some reason, the short boys were usually the ones asking me to dance.

While standing there with my black pumps on, that discomfort returned. I tried to slouch forward while watching the pool game, then pushed my glasses on my nose again. This habit seemed to surface, especially when nervous. Bill was staring me up and down.

Trying to keep my composure, while looking away, I blurted out a personal question. "Do you have a lady in your life?" That was unlike me to be so forward.

"Yes, I do. Her name is Karen. Karen Fisher. Been stayin' wit her bout a month."

Just then, a pang of jealousy went all through me. I knew Karen from school and never could understand what all the boys saw in her. She was a year older than I was and slept with so many boys. You would have thought that she was a queen from another country by her actions.

Karen, with her fiery temper and petite body, always had her nose in the air and ignored those less fortunate. Her short haircuts framed her pear-shaped face, which often contorted into an angry sneer. What Bill saw in her, bewildered me.

The Army granted her father an honorable discharge due to a service related incident. Because of the circumstances surrounding the matter, he received a check for the rest of his life. Therefore, he had a little money and was able to assist Karen financially. This helped her tremendously to be able to afford her own place and buy a vehicle.

Every time Karen crossed my path, she was clean. I always envied her extravagant lifestyle, which clearly showed by her expensive taste in clothes. It just seemed that Karen easily got the good things in life while I struggled to get even the simplest.

A moment later, Bill's partner approached us. He was strutting like a hard-core pimp. Bill introduced us, while touching my shoulder again. "Sarah, this is my cous, Carl Johnson. Carl, Sarah Jones."

Carl stepped forward to shake my hand. He stood two heads shorter with dark hair and dull brown eyes. His tacky clothing stacked loosely on his skinny frame. He reeked of alcohol.

"Hi, pleased to meet you," I said, shaking his limp hand, while taking a step backwards.

I quickly turned my attention back to Bill and asked, "How long will you be in town?"

"We're outa' here by tomorrow. You goin' be out later?"

"I plan to," I replied, while trying not to sound anxious.

"Well, gotta run now. Be back round nine. Wanna talk a little more then?"

I smiled. "Yeah, that sounds good."

After that, I went home to eat dinner. We had leftovers from the day before. Dinner consisted of shake and bake chicken, macaroni and cheese, and corn on the cob.

Cooking became my passion in my early teens. I watched numerous cooking shows on television and paid much attention to my mother cooking whenever possible. Creating recipes of my own was exciting. Adding another ingredient or two, and tasting the finished product, was a test in itself. Sometimes, it was downright good, and other times, my family would suddenly decide that a sandwich or a bowl of cereal would suffice. I caught the hint.

I had approximately three hours to kill time before going back to the "Riverview Bar." After dinner, Tina and I sat on the couch and watched a television show called, "The Animals Neighborhood." When that went off, we switched the channel to watch, "The Princess is Here." This was her favorite television program.

Close to the end of the day, Tina pulled out her coloring book and crayons and sat at the table. Soon it was time for her bath, and afterwards a snack. Most of the time, an ice cream cone was all she wanted.

The moment had come for me to start getting ready. I searched in my closet and decided to wear blue jeans, which complimented my matching blue and white poke-a-dot short-sleeve cotton blouse. My jeans had shrunk a little after the first wash, so they were a little bit high water. Two weeks ago, I had just purchased a new pair of white no-name brand tennis shoes. Choosing the right purse and costume jewelry was all I needed.

While taking my shower and getting dressed, my thoughts were about my new friend, possibly my "Mr. Right." I hoped to be the center of his attention when we meet up. Tonight would be the perfect opportunity to get the chance to know him and just maybe find out if the chemistry was mutual. Tomorrow would be my day off from work, which made it perfect for me to hang out.

By 8 p.m., I was completely dressed and ready to leave the house. Tina fell asleep as I read her a bedtime story.

I told mom not to wait up for me. My parents disliked my bar life. However, as long as my financial obligations had met their requirements and my chores were completed, I felt there should be no questions or demands about my activities. Besides, I am grown.

Whenever leaving the house to go out, my parents repeatedly told me to be careful and not to get into strangers' cars. Mom and dad prayed a lot and always asked the Lord for my safe return. Sometimes they would worry, but decided the best thing to do was to give me to the Lord. My mom stated that she refused to let me give her gray hairs before her time. It was a little too late for dad. His hair was already gray. Nevertheless, I felt "out of harm's way" and didn't have a care in the world.

CHAPTER TWO

THE NIGHT WAS RELATIVELY PEACEFUL. After leaving home, I looked up and prayed while remembering my parent's words. I asked God for his divine protection, and then ventured out into the streets. This had become a habit of added safety, since my mom and dad had already prayed. Once this happened, I felt ready for whatever came my way.

The closer I got to the bar, the noisier the night became. All of a sudden, somebody with a tan convertible drove pass me. The base of the music was extremely loud. I recognized one of my favorite songs, "The Closer I Get To Him." While listening, I began to wonder whether or not Bill would really show up or if he would have his woman by his side. Perhaps, my presence might be unnoticed. After all, he did seem popular.

It took me about twelve minutes to make it to the bar. Normally it takes approximately twenty minutes.

Upon entering the premises, I took a quick glance but did not see Bill. While repeatedly looking at my watch, realization hit me that it was still a little early, only about 8:45 p.m. I spoke to a couple of people, ordered a beer, and tried to relax and just be patient.

Since I was not a heavy drinker, this would probably last me half the night. Any indulging was merely to be sociable. The taste of beer or liquor never suited me. A second drink made me tipsy. After a third, I was as good as drunk.

Within my small network of friends, I trusted only a couple,

Simmone and Jannetta. Most of the time when hanging out, sitting alone was preferred rather than with a bunch of gossiping women. I hoped that no one would join me, which would give me an opportunity to have a few moments alone with Bill.

The time went from 9-10 p.m. Sitting unaccompanied too long, made me appear to be anti-sociable, so I got up and walked over to the jukebox. While skimming over the different selections, I noticed another one of my favorite songs, "Are You the One."

As I turned around to go back to my seat, Bobby walked in. Recently, I broke up with what he still called a relationship, and attempted to stay as far away from him as possible. This choice was not easy since almost every time I walked into the "Riverview Bar", he seemed to appear.

"Hey Girl," Bobby yelled.

"Hello Bobby." Seeing him frustrated me. I tried to ignore his hyperactive, arrogant, fast-talking self, but nothing worked. 6 ft., "Fast Talking Bobby", continued running his mouth.

He was very bowlegged and not a bad looking man at all. I loved his style of matching clothing, including the cap on his head. Not only did he talk fast, but he walked swiftly as well. His identical twin brother, who was never too far behind, had most of the same characteristics as Bobby.

Bobby had been living with his girlfriend, Sheila, for years. That's why I never took our relationship too seriously.

"What's up, Sarah?"

"Nothing!" I muttered. Because of his notoriety as a fast smooth talker, you had to listen to him attentively. If you didn't, you would have a hard time understanding what he was trying to say.

Bobby ordered his favorite drink, gin with orange juice. Then he bought me a drink, rum, and coke. My unattended beer was still sitting at the table.

I took a few sips and began to feel tipsy. When Bobby turned his head, I slyly poured the rest on the floor. Nobody was watching.

Since the opportunity presented itself, there would be no better time than the present to get it over with and resolve the so-called relationship with Bobby. I had a buzz.

Boldly, I babbled, "Look, 'Mr. Stutter Box', this relationship ain't working out. I have finally seen the light, you dig, you ole' arrogant player. Why you all up in my face anyway? If you think I'm gonna continue being your sidekick, you must be out of your toe-pickin' mind. For the last time, it's over and I ain't waitin' till no fat lady sing!"

Bobby looked shocked and mesmerized for about five seconds. Obviously, he did everything possible to keep from making a scene. However, his mouth flew wide open as if to say, *I know you didn't go there!*

He bent over, gritted his teeth, and whispered in my ear, "Girl, step outside a minute. We need to talk!"

I hesitated. Bobby grabbed my hand and took me to the nearest alley. His demeanor suddenly changed as his true colors came out. He told me completely off.

"Now don't you start acting simple again. Every time you get mad and can't have your way, you want to break up!"

Bobby pointed his finger in my face and continued stuttering. "Do you know what your problem is, huh? You are just too sensitive and insecure. If I didn't care about you, I would have kicked you to the curb a long time ago. And don't you ever say that mess to me again, you understand!"

His manipulations did not scare me at all. I decided not to respond, but under my breath, I called him a "Butthead"! It made no sense for me to argue with him. No matter what I said, he was good for fast-talking me and having said the last word. Shutting my mouth was the wisest thing to do at the time. Besides, I had already given him a piece of my mind. Moments later, he calmed down. We walked back to the bar and then he left.

As I contemplated on leaving, Bill and Carl surprisingly entered the bar. I looked at the clock on the wall. The time was 11 p.m. Bill immediately walked over to me with a puzzled look on his face and said, "Yo, I thought you said you ain't had no man!"

"I ain't!" I replied.

"Sho look like it to me. I saw y'all holdin' hands."

"It ain't like that. Talk what you know. Matter of fact, that's a done deal!"

"Yeah, right!" Bill retorted, rolling his eyes. Then he stared at me and asked, "Are you okay?" I guess my words slurred just a little.

Bill didn't seem to believe me concerning Bobby. There was no need to try to convince him otherwise. We talked for about ten more minutes, and then Bill walked away while I was in the middle of a sentence.

Not long after that, his woman, Karen, came in. I should have known. They talked for a few moments before leaving the bar together. I looked around to see if anyone noticed how he played me. They did.

Right away, pimp-walking Carl came over to me and asked, "What a good lookin' girl like you doin' wit out a man?" I believe he contemplated getting my attention off Bill and Karen.

"I guess I ain't got what it takes."

Carl took that statement as an invitation. "Well, you mind if I buy a nice lady a drink?"

"No thanks," I shouted. "I'm through drinking for the night."

After ordering a drink for himself, Carl staggered wide legged and sat right next to me. With his wine smelling breath in my face, he said, "Hey, maybe we can do sometin' when I come back. I sho would like to get to know you better, pretty lady and all that."

Slobber leaked from the corner of his mouth as he tried to reach over and kiss me. I was flabbergasted and quickly turned my face. Then, he had the audacity to put his sweaty palms on my right thigh. With a mean look on my face, I snatched his hand away and got ready to give him a piece of my mind when my brother Mark walked in. As I stood up, slobbering Carl got up, gulped the last of his drink and left.

Mark and I were two years apart. He rarely hung out in bars, but occasionally came to buy a forty-ounce bottle of beer. My brother preferred to drink at home or go to a friend's house. He married a nice woman, Latisha, who was about fifteen years older than he was. They lived fairly close to our parents.

Mark wore thick glasses and had somewhat of a potbelly. I guess drinking beer had a lot to do with his oversize stomach. He was about 5' 11", had round shoulders, and weighed about 180 pounds. He had a jerry curl, but mostly wore it straight back into a ponytail.

He never questioned me, but I believe Mark felt some type of way about me hanging in bars. Frequently, he passed by me while going to play his numbers. He always wanted to know what time I was going home.

My brother's passion was playing the lottery and watching football on television.

"Hi, Sarah."

"Hi, Mark, you don't have to work today?" He worked as a laborer at the Cantonian Steel Mill.

"No, I just finished up midnight this morning. I got lucky and hit the numbers today. I played 636, my house number. Unfortunately, I boxed it instead of playing it straight. The number man just paid me my money so I stopped here to get me a forty-ounce bottle of beer, and then I'm heading on home. What about you? How long are you staying out?"

"Well, I was just leaving. Can you ride me home?" The rain had just started, and I did not want to get drenched.

"Of course," Mark said. "It is getting rather late for you to have to walk up that hill by yourself anyway."

There was no reason for me to stay out because Bill had already left.

The next day, I took my daughter, Tina, shopping. We went to our favorite place, "Seventh Avenue Clothing Store". I bought Tina four outfits, which consisted of two pantsuits and two dresses. After that, we went to the shoe store. She tried on several pairs due to her wide feet. After spending about an hour in the store, we were satisfied with two cute pair of sandals. She could wear them with her new outfits.

As we were leaving the shoe store, Tina said, "I'm hungry, Mommy."

"Okay honey, let's go across the street, and get you a 'happy meal'. I'm a little hungry too." After getting our bellies full, we were both tired and ready to go home. I needed to get plenty of rest for work the next day.

Before my employment at "Baker's Steel Mill," the company was in the midst of incorporating a new policy. Management was required to hire a certain percentage of women. I filled out an application, had an interview, and was among the second group of women hired. The different positions filled included labor, utility, and coke-oven cleaner. I trained on all three.

As the years progressed, those that were skilled taught me how to run the "Door Machine," the "Larry Car," the "Pusher," and the "Hot Car." My superiors stated my performance was diligent and outstanding. On occasion, I had the opportunity to be the "Gang Leader". This position designated a person to relieve the machine operators for their breaks.

The times I operated the machines was usually because of crew call-offs due to bad weather. These positions paid more. However, I was somewhat nervous because of the increased responsibilities. For example, if someone on the "Door Machine" or the "Pusher" accidently dropped the door, it would take some time to get this problem fixed. The machine called the "Hot Car" would be an issue in itself if someone missed the load of coke coming out. In either case, the temporary shutdown of the batteries meant a loss of time and money for the company, which would most likely cause the person that made the mistake to be wrote up. Cases like these flooded the place with all kind of authority figures. My regular job was definitely my preference. It was less demanding and stressful.

My attire in the mill consisted of black hard-toe boots, a yellow work uniform, a respirator, and work gloves. We also had to wear a hard hat, goggles, and a pair of long johns underneath our uniform to protect us from the heat or burns from the hot coal. I felt twenty-five or more pounds heavier when completely in uniform.

Even though my plans did not include making a career out of this job, whenever the opportunity came, I would double out or work on my off days. My take home pay was "sweet".

After working for almost three years and having good reviews, the personnel department considered me for a promotion to a supervisor's position. I was astonished, and took a couple of days to think it over. I decided the responsibilities would be too stressful and turned it down. My sanity was more important.

Other than my job, life went on as usual. I wondered how long it would be before I saw Bill again. He seemed to have vanished. I heard he had left town.

CHAPTER THREE

I DECIDED TO TAKE A WALK downtown trying to forget Bill ever existed. Moments later, someone blew a horn. I turned around and coincidently there they were. Bill was driving Karen's three-year-old 1975 Lincoln Continental. I checked it out thoroughly.

The exterior color was a charcoal grey, and the body seemed to be in good condition. Apparently, somebody gave it a good wax job. The interior of the roomy vehicle had grey leather seats and no scuffs or imperfections were visible. All I noticed was a hubcap missing from the back tire.

"Hey girl, what up?" Bill said.

Trying not to divulge the fact of missing him, I said, "Hello, I didn't think you were coming back. How long will you be here this time?"

"For a minute, feel like hangin'?"

"Sure!" I was delighted that he asked me. Carl's refusal to budge from the front seat, gave me no choice but to get in the back. We rode around for about an hour. Being around Bill helped me to become familiar with his lifestyle. At times, he would crack a joke, which wasn't always funny. Carl would burst out laughing, so I did too.

"How's your family?" I asked.

"They all okay, but my raise not feelin'well. Guess she got that bug that's goin' round. I told her to see the doctor, but she's hardheaded. She probably thinks that bug will just take its course. I imagine she'll be fine in about a week."

20

We talked about the rest of the family. I was shocked to hear him say his mother was hardheaded.

Carl had very few words to say the entire time we were in the car. His personality seemed diverse and somewhat on the quiet side when he was sober. I could handle that. In fact, friendship with Carl might inadvertently be to my advantage. As long as we were cool, perhaps, it would give me more opportunities to be around Bill. They were usually together.

Every time Carl wanted to hang out with me, I would pull Bill to the side. "Hey Bill, Carl just asked me to go to the disco with him tonight. If you are free, why don't you come along?"

"Well, I ain't tryin' to get in y'alls way. Carl might wanna be alone wit you. He acts like he's crushin' on you anyway."

"Oh, please. I doubt that very much. He's just trying to be sociable."

Most of the time, Bill could be convinced into coming along when he wasn't extremely busy. I enjoyed his company. He was so cool.

Every time we went to a disco, I had a ball. Carl was a lousy dancer, but so was I. Bill, on the other hand, was a stunning dancer, and caught everyone's attention. All the single women in the house observed his unique style and seemed to wait in line just for the opportunity to dance with him. When my turn came, I was stiff as a board. Having a drink or two would sometimes loosen me up.

Everybody appeared to be doing a dance called the "bump", except for me. I felt like an unbendable penguin moving from side to side. There was no rhythm in my body, whatsoever. When Bill would bump one way, my body would unintentionally go in the opposite direction. All of a sudden, he would change partners. It made me feel awkward standing alone on the dance floor with nobody coming my way to collaborate with me except Carl.

Bill's presence always seemed to perk me up. I wanted the opportunity to get to know him a little better. There was just something about him. My opinion of him thus far was that he was calm, cool, collective, and a little wild at times—especially when he had those dark sunglasses on. They seemed to boost his character in a similar way the "wild wig" boosted mine. Entertaining others seems to be a piece of cake for Bill.

Socializing with Carl seemed more like a task. We never had anything interesting to say to each other. Whenever Carl left the scene, I would ask Bill if everything was okay. He seemed to have a lot on his mind. I was concerned.

At times, he would say, "Yeah, I'm fine." Then later one day he surprised me and asked, "You got some doe I can borrow? I'm broke and hate to walk round wit no money. I'll give it back."

I thought it was strange for him to ask me for money. He had given me the impression that everything was under control including being the man. However, it was not a problem lending Bill a few bucks. If he forgot about paying me back, that would have been okay too.

I responded right away. "I do have a few dollars on me. How much do you need?" He boldly requested a loan of ten dollars. I reached into my purse and gave it to him. This was probably chump change to him, but he thanked me anyway for being a true friend.

"Don't worry about it. That's what friends are for," I said. Later on, I overheard him talking with Carl about his birthday coming up in about a week and a half.

Carl, on the other hand, never asked me for anything except to hang out. Usually he wanted to take me to a disco, concert, or to the park to hear a band. I would stall from giving him an answer until I found out if Bill would be joining us. If not, I made excuses not to go. Unfortunately, Carl was just not my type.

"I'm sorry, Carl. I appreciate you asking me and would love to go, but I just remembered something. I'm supposed to take Tina to a birthday party around the same time. Sorry, maybe next time."

Carl looked somewhat disappointed as he rolled his beady eyes at me and said, "Whatever!"

I'm sure he was tired of all the excuses. I refused to get into any dialogue with him over the matter, so I said goodnight and went home.

The next day, my work shift was 4 p.m. to12 a.m. I decided to get up early and take Tina shopping. After breakfast, we rushed down the street to catch the 48-C bus to the mall.

As I contemplated on where to go first, my attention suddenly turned towards "Mathew and Luke's Clothing Store." In the window appeared a sharp, brown, and blue jean leather suit. The two-piece vest and matching pair of pants was very distinctive. Part of the outfit was genuine leather. The other piece was a cotton blue-jean material. Oh, how I just loved it! A few moments went by as I pondered in my mind how good it would look on Bill.

Tina looked up and said, "Mommy, you goin' buy dis for Grandpap?" She knew Sunday was Father's Day.

"No, Honey. I'm just admiring the way the outfit is made. It is very different." After much thought, my final decision was to get it for Bill as a gift. The exact date of his birthday was unknown to me, but I knew it would be soon because of over hearing his conversation with Carl.

I only had enough money to spend on Tina that day. She always wanted a rocking horse. We went into several different stores and finally found one on sale for $79.00. It was quite heavy, but I managed to drag it on the bus.

Tina was so excited. She couldn't wait to get home. When she did, she rocked for what seemed like hours on that horse. It practically made me dizzy just watching her move back and forth. However, it made my day just to put a smile on her face.

The following week, I returned to "Mathew and Luke's Clothing Store" and purchased the suit for Bill. It was still on sale. On my way home, I wondered where to hide it until Bill's birthday. I decided to keep it underneath my bed with a cover on it, hopeful that no one would find it and start asking me questions.

For the next three days, I went through the routine of sneaking the outfit in and out of the house. Catching up with Bill seemed almost impossible. Finally, there was a glimpse of him standing on the corner by the bar. Approaching him had to be quick before he disappeared.

"Hey Bill, do you have a minute? I need to talk to you. It won't take long, I promise."

He seemed a little hesitant as if waiting for someone or something. Then he swaggered over to me with a grim look on his face. I did not want to prolong him from whatever he was trying to do.

"Bill, I have a surprise for you." I gave him the shopping bag. He didn't hesitate to look inside.

He smiled and said, "What up wit this?"

I smiled back. "I heard you say that you had a birthday coming up so I bought you a gift. 'Happy Birthday'! I hope it fits." "Could you please do me a favor and not tell Carl?"

Bill looked startled, yet pleased. "You got it. And thanks for the gift." Then he disappeared into the crowd.

That same night Carl started acting indifferent towards me. He would barely speak and never asked me out again. I never meant to hurt his feelings.

A couple of weeks later, Bill offered to walk me home from the bar. I was astonished. He stated it was entirely too late for me to be walking up the hill alone. As we got closer to the house, I thanked him and turned around to say goodbye. He caught me by surprise as he put his arms around me and kissed me. I was shocked. Bill had never approached me in that way.

"I'll ring you later," he said, while walking away.

I stood on my parents' porch stunned and in a daze. Closing my eyes and taking a fresh breath of air allowed my imagination to get the best of me. I decided it was time to go in.

As I entered the house, Tina ran and gave me a big hug. She had waited up for me. "Hi Mommy, guess what? I ate all my food!"

"You did!" I said. "What did you have?"

"Granny fix me chicken, rice, and Popeye's spinach," said happy Tina.

This was a big deal to Tina since she never really cared for vegetables. I gave her a big hug and said, "Mommy is so proud of you, and since you have been such a good girl, I'm going to have a really big surprise for you this weekend. I can't tell you now or it won't be a surprise."

Her eyes got big, and she had that wide grin on her face again. I sat on the recliner and put Tina on my lap. She was already in her pajamas and ready for bed.

Dad had gone to night service at the church, so I sat up and talked to Mom. For the most part, I kept my relationships pretty much a secret. I knew that if the man weren't a churchgoer, my parents would have given me the third degree.

Mom always told me not to ever let a man use me and not to bring any more babies into this world unless I was married. She said if I continued to be disobedient, I would reap what I sow.

Mom and I had our fallouts. At times, I thought she was just plain mean. Her way of looking out for my best interest was not the way I perceived it. However, not wanting to see me hurt or destroy my life kept momma on her knees.

Tina had fallen asleep on my lap, so I took her upstairs to bed. By the time I came back downstairs, the "Gospel Show" was on. I decided to watch it with my mom. Her favorite singers were on.

Dad finally came in. I asked him, "How was service?"

"It was a blessing to be in the house of the Lord. You should have been there. We had a good time. Brother Henson spoke tonight about faithfulness. Three souls came to the Lord."

I could tell Dad was getting ready to witness to me again. I yawned, stood up, and headed upstairs to watch the television in my bedroom. It was 10 p.m. "Goodnight, mom and dad."

"Goodnight Sarah." Then dad said, "You can run, but you can't hide."

I pretended not to hear that remark. I knew something about Jesus, but was not ready for all that religion.

About an hour later, mom and dad came up the steps to bed. Around 11:30 p.m., my telephone rang. I quickly answered it on the first ring to keep from disturbing Tina as well as my parents.

"Hello," I whispered.

It was Bill. "Hey! Sorry to ring you so late, but I need a big favor."

Before I could respond, Bill said, "Need twenty bucks. Been gamblin' and losin' like crazy. Twenty bucks would put me back in the game. I'm gonna win in the next one, you watch and see. After that, if you can get back out, goin' try to get Karen's car so we can shoot the breeze. Gotta be back by mornin' though, to take her to work."

My plans to be in for the night suddenly changed. "Sure, I can spare twenty dollars. How long will you be?" I did not want to fight sleep half the night waiting for him.

"Not long. Be there in a minute. I will sho nough pay you back. I'm leavin' now, so be standin' outside."

I threw on some clothes, grabbed my jacket, and tiptoed down the stairs. Disturbing my parents would have resulted in listening to another lecture.

25

Bill pulled up and I gave him the money. He told me to be ready in an hour and quickly pulled off.

I took a quick shower and was dressed in thirty minutes. Leaving a note on my bed would be the right thing to do, just in case daybreak arrived before my return. I assumed we were going to an all-night disco but stated in the note that I would be at the bowling alley. My younger sister, Lorraine would see to Tina if she woke up before my return.

Lorraine was fifteen going on sixteen years of age. She knew a little about Bill from ease dropping on my conversations on the phone. I tried to hide as much as possible for fear of her "blabber mouthing" to mom and dad whatever she knew.

Lorraine resembled me but had a lighter complexion. She was about an inch shorter than I was. She had thin hair just like mom and loved wearing her hair in a ponytail. Lorraine walked with a slight limp due to a fall from breaking her leg a year ago. Mom and dad were not as strict with her like the rest of us. She got away with things that we couldn't.

Lorraine would always give you her last if she could, but if you get on her bad side, she would most certainly tell you off. I always told her, though, that her "bark was bigger than her bite."

Just then, the phone rang again. It was about time. I had been waiting for an hour and a half.

Before I could say hello, he said, "Yo, come out now. I'm on my way."

His speech sounded a little slurred. I hoped he had not been drinking. Five minutes later, he pulled up! While getting into the car, I knew right away.

Glancing at him, I asked, "Are you all right?"

"Yeah babe, had some beers, that's all. I won forty dollars plus your twenty back, bought us some weed too."

After looking at Bill, I became a little leery and kept my eye on him. He drove okay.

"Why'd you do that? I don't want to smoke." I was becoming disappointed about the night's beginning and wondered if it would get better.

Bill said, "Since you wit me, we might as well party."

Hanging out was not the problem. Partying was just not on my agenda. I would have been content going to a disco or just riding around, enjoying the breeze, and talking.

"Where are we going?" I asked reluctantly.

"We're going to see Mo."

"Mo who?" I said, looking dumbfounded.

Bill looked at me and laughed. "The motel, Sarah, just us. Don't act stupid now. You know what up."

Now, I realized his intention, unready for this, nor was I the kind of girl who would do such a thing so soon. Getting to know him better was on my agenda. Things were just happening too fast. I liked Bill a lot, but did not know him that well to be going to a motel. *Would he still respect me? Was I in any kind of danger?* All these questions were in my mind. I was too embarrassed to ask him to take me home, so I said absolutely nothing. A silent little prayer helped me tremendously.

CHAPTER FOUR

THE DURATION OF THE RIDE SEEMED endless, but finally we arrived at the "Shady Hady Motel." It was a small, rundown place located on the outskirts of town. As we stood at the front desk, Bill grabbed my hand. He pulled out identification and registered us under the name of Mr. and Mrs. Darnell Simpson. I turned my head after noticing the rolls of quarters and dimes he pulled out to pay for the room. It totally blew me away for a moment-- including the fact that he used a fake I.D. The elderly woman behind the desk gave us the key to room 19. I was beginning to get nervous again, so I said another quiet prayer.

The musty smell of the room hit me when Bill opened the door. A dim table lamp added a somber effect to the dark curtains and faded blue bed covers. The atmosphere was dull. Unlike me, Bill paid no attention to his surroundings.

Taking his jacket off and acting as if he was home seemed satisfactory to him as he pulled out a six-pack of beer. He could have taken me to a better place than this.

Bill immediately began drinking can after can of beer. He handed me one, and I slowly drank about half of it. It did help me to loosen up a little. Then Bill went in his pocket, pulled out a joint, and lit it. The horrible smell signified that it was more than just weed. I didn't want any part of that and hoped he wouldn't pass it my way. Lucky for me, he decided not to share. I would have refused it anyway. The odor became so overbearing that I turned on the air conditioner hoping it might suck in some of the smell. It did.

All of a sudden, Bill seemed very talkative. He told me some more jokes. This time, they were funny. He also talked about his childhood and some of his interests. He never finished school but claimed he maintained average grades and received his G.E.D. He chatted about getting his life together and pursuing a career as a professional comedian. I was impressed and therefore encouraged him about pursuing his goals.

I knew many people who were down on their luck or out in the streets only to make a comeback. Some became very successful in their careers. That's why I would never try to underestimate his ability to change.

As his conversation ceased, I began to drift but became alert as he put his gentle arms around me. Next, he tried to seduce me. I stood firm and resisted. Bill was a likeable person, but I was just not ready. Finally, he fell asleep while his loud snoring kept me awake. Before long, it was daybreak and time to go.

On the way home, his few words made me a little uneasy. I assumed Bill was not a morning person and maybe still tired.

We were back at our destination in no time. Bill dropped me off at home and went to pick up Karen to take her to work.

At home, I tiptoed up the steps and headed straight to bed. Tina would be waking up in a couple of hours wanting to play.

Four days later, Bill called. I gave him the benefit of the doubt but thought he could have at least called me the next day. However, the short conversation puzzled me.

Eventually, I ran into him at the bar. To my astonishment, he sat alone. Not quite knowing what his reaction would be, I pulled up a chair and sat directly across from him.

"Bill, I had a great time with you the other night and enjoyed our conversation." I hoped he felt the same.

Instead of responding right away, he stared at his mug of beer for a moment and blurted, "Karen was noided when I took her to work that mornin'."

"About what?" I knew she wouldn't be too happy since Bill had been out with her car all night, but I thought I'd ask anyway.

"She wanna know where I was at wit her car. I told her, I was gambling wit my homies." His mouth turned up in a crooked smile as his eyes met mine.

He continued, "Don't mess wit me! I'm already mad cause I been losin' my money all night." He laughed viciously. His brown eyes gleamed, as he seemed to enjoy a sense of power.

"What did she say after that?" I asked, while watching to get his reaction concerning Karen's anger. His persona seemed to change.

"She wasn't feelin' it, but knew not to open her mouth. She ain't dumb."

I nodded, pretending to be in agreement with him and glad that Bill put Karen in her place.

Bill's attention quickly turned toward Carl as he entered the bar. Carl joined us for a moment but totally ignored me. I wondered if Bill informed him about us being at the motel. It was really none of his business and wished he hadn't come to sit with us. Spending a little time with Bill, without interruption, would have made my day.

I was glad that someone started playing some really soft and mellow music on the jukebox. My thoughts were about the quality time previously spent with Bill. I felt that we were getting closer. Bill, on the other hand, never mentioned it. It certainly would have put my mind at ease just to know how he felt.

Our conversation ended quickly. Bill got up and exited the bar with Carl without saying a word to me--not even a goodbye. His rude actions were very disappointing, so I left the bar and walked home. While thinking about the whole scenario, I came up with all kind of excuses for his behavior.

Maybe if I fixed myself up, he would pay more attention to me. As soon as I get home, this silly wig is coming off and I'm doing something to my hair. I had previously purchased a relaxer a couple of weeks ago.

Upon my arrival at home, no one was there. While being appreciative for the privacy, I headed straight to my room to lie across my bed. My feelings for Bill were growing while hoping he would not give up on me. Maybe, some day, we would get to spend quality time with each other again.

All of a sudden, someone came in the house. Hastily, I got up and saw that it was my sister, Lorraine, along with a few of her friends. Just then, it dawned on me that today was Lorraine's birthday. She had just turned sixteen. Mom told her that she could invite a few friends to the house for a sleepover.

Because of my being in my own little world, it completely slipped my mind about her birthday. Something needed to be done and speedily. I went downstairs, gave her a hug, and pretended to be waiting for her arrival.

"Happy Birthday Lorraine! I'm planning to cook you and your friends something special for your sweet-sixteenth birthday celebration. Just give me two hours and I promise that you will have an all-you-can-eat grand buffet from Sarah's kitchen."

"Thank you!" Lorraine giggled.

I picked up the phone and called my brother, Mark. Luckily, he was home. "Mark, could you please do me a big favor and go to the grocery store for me? I'll pay you when you get here."

"Dog girl, I was just leavin' out to go play my numbers." Then he grumbled. "What do you want?" If there is one thing I can say about my brother, he may grumble and mumble, but he would do whatever he could to help his family.

"I need a 2 lb. bag of cooked shrimp, 10 lbs. of chicken wings, a 2 lb. box of macaroni, 5 cans of evaporated milk, and 6 cups of sharp cheddar shredded cheese, 3 cups of mozzarella cheese, 1 lb. box of linguine noodles, 3 tomatoes, and 3 cucumbers. Everything else is already here. Oh, I almost forgot! Pick up a case of canned pop. It doesn't matter what kind. Try not to go over fifty dollars because that's all I can afford to spend."

"Dog girl, I don't have fifty dollars on me and you need to write a list because I am not going to remember all that stuff!"

This slightly changed my plans to be on time. He had to come and get the money and the list from me before going to the store.

In the mean time, two pots of water were on the stove, waiting to boil. I opened up a large can of green beans, dumped the contents in another pot, poured a little bacon grease in it, and seasoned the vegetables. The oil heated up in the deep fryer while the seasoned flour was ready for the chicken.

It was now time to put the rice in one of the boiling pots of water to simmer for twenty minutes. By the time Mark came back from the store, things were well organized, and the rest of the cooking began. I thanked Mark and gave him a few extra dollars for his pocket.

The meal took a little bit longer than expected. The menu consisted of fried chicken, baked macaroni and cheese, linguine salad, shrimp scampi over rice, and green beans. Mom and dad purchased the cake and ice cream earlier.

While preparing the meal, Lorraine and her friends were playing the radio and dancing as if they knew how. They were laughing and having a good "ole time." One person was constantly peeking out the window on the lookout for dad's car pulling up. Lorraine and I knew our parents did not allow such non-Christian music playing in their home.

After two hours of fun-filled entertainment along with dancing, dad's car finally pulled up. Someone turned the radio off, and I cut the TV on. A western was on Channel 7, and everyone quickly sat down pretending to be watching a "Cowboy Indian" movie.

Mom and dad came in. After a few moments, they joined us. We knew dad enjoyed watching his westerns.

Dinner was now ready. One by one, we got up and fixed our plates. Everyone ate until full.

Lorraine and her friends complimented the meal. "It was all that and worth the wait." Afterwards, we put the leftover food away and cleaned the kitchen. Lorraine and her guests played board games in the dining room.

Tina and I quietly went upstairs to our room. I had enough excitement for the day and was too tired to perm my hair that night. After our baths, we went straight to bed. I closed the door, cut the television off, and the rest was history.

That night I had the weirdest dream about someone knocking on my door. Without looking to see who it was, I opened it. A man stood there, but I was unable to make out the face. He asked me for something. I immediately sensed danger and quickly tried to shut the door. His strength "over powered" me, the door flew open, and he came in. No one seemed to hear me screaming to the top of my lungs. When Tina started moving around in the bed, I woke up from this dream. My heart was beating fast. I sat straight up and looked at the clock. It was only 2 a.m.

Questions went through my mind. *What did this dream mean? Was it a warning sign for me?* Fear set in because the dream seemed to come out of nowhere. Unable to go back to sleep, I got up and sat at the table in the corner of my bedroom and began to write. Writing seemed to give me a sense of peace. Therefore, I began a poem entitled:

Rescue Me

One day as I was sitting,

Beneath the apple tree,

I looked up to the heavens,

Lonely as could be,

Asking God a question,

What is wrong with me?

Tired of making bad choices,

Come and rescue me.

I thought I heard Him say,

If you listen to the wind,

And look up at the stars,

Something deep within,

Will catch you if you fall.

After the finished writing, I felt so much better. There seemed to be a mystifying sense of peace within me. I left the poem on the table and returned to bed.

The next morning, realization hit me that maybe I shouldn't have eaten all that food before going to bed. I placed the poem in my drawer with the rest of my previous writings.

When Tina woke up, we went downstairs. Lorraine's company was all over the living room floor in their sleeping bags. The smell of fresh coffee woke everyone up. Mom was already in the kitchen making grits, scrambled eggs, home fries, and sausage. The homemade syrup simmered while the country style biscuits were in the oven. The aroma of breakfast filled the atmosphere.

After the delicious breakfast, I went back upstairs to put the much-needed perm in my hair. That "wild wig" will not be on my head this weekend. My birthday is coming up in two weeks, and I wanted to look good.

When Friday came around, I arrived at the bar around 7 p.m. Although a sense of rejection from Bill happened previously, I was still hoping to see him and even more determined to spend my birthday with him.

CHAPTER FIVE

THE VERY NEXT FRIDAY, I REMAINED in the bar until closing. Bill never showed up. A few people chatted with me while I kept a keen eye on the door. Being able to get a glimpse of Carl would have meant Bill was close by.

The next day, around noon, my phone rang. I ran upstairs and answered it on the second ring. It was not Bill, but my friend, Jannetta. I rushed her off the phone trying not to miss my important phone call. Ten minutes later, the phone rang again. I hustled back upstairs. It was Simmone. She needed to vent about something that happened on her job. At this particular time, I really didn't want to hear it and rudely hung the phone up on her. As I was about half way down the stairs, the phone rang once again. By this time, I was huffing and puffing.

"Hello!" I said rather sharply.

"Hey girl, don't know what's goin' on, but you been on my mind. Wanna go to lunch, my treat?"

As I caught my breath, I started to ask, "Are we going to the 'Burger or the Hot Dog Joint'?" I never forgot about the cheap motel he took me to.

Instead, I said, "That's very nice of you. Sure, I'd love to go." I had to be careful not to sound too excited.

"Good, meet me bout an hour, and we'll go someplace nice. Gotta get a ride."

His efforts delighted me. Finally, we would get another chance to spend some quality time together in spite of his penny-pinching ways. In addition, it would give me the opportunity to mention my up-coming birthday.

My house chores were quickly finished. Mom was not feeling well, so I declined from asking her to babysit. Since Lorraine wasn't home, Tina would have to go with me. This would give me a chance to see his reaction towards her. Bill had met her previously but never had a chance to get to know her.

As I arrived at my destination, Bill was waiting for me. He clowned as we sat on the bench, which helped me to see a fun-loving side of him. He played with Tina, made her laugh, and acted like a big kid. Their interaction with each other made my day.

Bill manipulated Karen to get her car again and took us to a restaurant called "Bigmomma's Place," which was approximately seven miles away. I had heard about it, but never had the pleasure of dining there. The address was 235 8th St., located in a small town called Westport. When we pulled up, Bill told us to wait in the car. He came back out with two red roses. He handed one to both of us. I thought that was so sweet of him. Tina looked at me and giggled. He had purchased the roses from the flower shop located next door to the restaurant.

Opening the car door for us was not on his agenda that particular day. Instead, he motioned for us to get out. *Some gentleman*, I thought. As we walked into the restaurant, I expected to see a bunch of fat women because of the name of the restaurant. Instead, a rather tall and medium-built middle-aged woman came to greet us. She was very kind and handed us a menu.

While glancing around, I noticed the atmosphere was quite different from any other restaurant I had ever been to. There was a big screen television with a VCR. A gospel choir in the video was "throwing down" and "rocking the house." People were shouting, *Glory Hallelujah!* Bill grabbed my arm and escorted me to our table with Tina following behind.

As I looked around, a blackboard hung up on one side of the wall. The special of the day was meatloaf, mashed potatoes/gravy, green beans, and a roll, all for $2.29. Next to the menu was another chalkboard that said, **Food For Thought.** The scripture quoted from the bible mesmerized me:

Psalm 88:1-3

O Lord God of my salvation, I have
cried day and night before thee: Let my
prayer come before thee: incline thine
ear unto my cry; For my soul is full of
troubles: and my life draweth nigh unto
the grave.

I read my bible on occasion but had very little understanding
of what the scriptures meant.

While pondering on the verses, two servers came out from the
back. They both wore a very bright African-colored apron with a
matching hat and scarf. One server brought out dessert and placed it
on the counter. The other asked us what we wanted to drink while we
were looking over the menu. Before I could answer, Bill spoke up
and ordered us all a glass of water.

There was something cool about this restaurant. It must have
been the atmosphere because nothing significantly glamorous stood
out. There were ten round tables at the most, each seating four
people. The white walls looked freshly painted, but the hardwood
floors needed a wax job. I could tell the counters were not finished,
that's about it.

Everyone seemed so nice and friendly. Because of Bill's
lifestyle, I was astonished that he brought me into a Christian
restaurant. From previous conversations, I was under the impression
that he didn't believe in God.

Several other customers came into the restaurant. A few sat
to dine in, but most of them had take-outs. While looking over the
lunch and dinner menu, I noticed on the back that one could get
breakfast at any time of the day. The hours of operation were
Monday thru Saturday from 11 a.m.to 6 p.m. This restaurant had a
reputation of down-to-earth southern food.

We were now ready to order our meal. Tina wanted a kid's
meal, which consisted of chicken nuggets, French fries, applesauce,
and a drink. Three chicken wings and one side of macaroni and
cheese was my order. I didn't know Bill's money situation and he
never told me to get whatever I wanted.

After the server wrote down what we wanted, Bill asked for the works; Barbecue ribs, fried chicken, potato salad, macaroni and cheese, fresh collard greens, yams, black-eyed peas and corn bread. Then he requested a bowl of banana pudding for dessert.

I loved banana pudding and wanted some too, but reluctant to speak up. Bill didn't offer. When the server approached Tina and me for our dessert selection, I politely said, "No thank you."

While patiently waiting for our food, Bill pulled out a pocket full of money and started counting it. This was my first time witnessing him having so much cash while wondering where it all came from. I hoped that he hit the lottery instead of the possibility of him doing something illegal. Focusing on the television played a big part in me pretending not to see all that money.

"Hey Bill, that was nice of you to bring us here. I can't wait to see what the food taste like."

"All for you. I knew y'all would like it. You been so nice. I think you gonna be alright for me."

"Thank you!" I smiled and decided this was the perfect time to mention about my upcoming birthday. "My birthday is next week, August 3rd. Do you think maybe we could do something together? I enjoy being around you and wouldn't want to spend it with anyone else. I know you're busy. That's why I'm asking you ahead of time."

"Can't see why not, where you wanna go?"

"It doesn't matter, whatever you decide." He smiled and I was glad he didn't say he would be busy.

Our meal came out not long after our conversation. The food was great. Bill ate enough to feed a family of four. He was devouring his meal and smacking his lips. I pretended not to notice his bad manners. Tina stared at him with disbelief. When Bill finished eating, he gave a loud belch without saying, "Excuse me".

Tina thought that to be very funny and laughed aloud. I was so embarrassed. Some of the other customer's were snickering. I am glad no one knew me.

After everyone had finished eating, he paid the bill and left a 50-cent tip. I reached into my purse and left a few more dollars once Bill walked away.

On the way home, I said, "Thank you for such a nice outing. I really enjoyed myself."

"Good, enjoyed the evenin' myself. When is your birthday again?"

"Next Saturday. This will be a busy week for me, so I won't be back out until Friday. You can pick me up around 8, if that's okay with you."

Bill winked.

We pulled up in front of my house and said our goodbyes. Bill touched my hand, reached over, and kissed me on the cheek. Tina giggled.

I went into the house and couldn't wait for our next date. I began prancing, dancing, and singing around the house. I visualized finally finding my "Mister Right."

Dad asked, "Are you okay?"

"Oh, I'm fine. I found someone I really like, and he feels the same about me."

"Well you better know what you're doing."

Dad looked at me sternly. "What do you know about this man? Does he go to church? Does he have a job? Does he have an education?"

My dad just had to go there. "He's a very nice person, and he does a lot of things." I ended the conversation by pretending to have to go to the bathroom.

This was another sign to keep my feelings to myself. No matter whom I dated, my parents always found something negative to say. I'm sure they would have been more than pleased if I dated an usher or choirboy from the church. I liked Bill, and nobody is going to change how I feel.

My shift was 4 p.m. to 12 a.m. that week. The days just seemed to fly. When Friday came around, I paid Lorraine to help keep an eye on Tina, so mom could get a break. Around 6 p.m., I started getting ready and chose a tan pantsuit made out of polyester material. The slacks contrasted my black sandals, which had a one-inch heel.

My perm was fresh which made my hair nice and straight. Loraine styled it into a French roll. The dangling earrings purchased from the discount store finished my appearance.

When Bill came to pick me up, he blew the horn. He was looking like a handsome "Super-Fly." He had on the blue jean leather outfit that I bought him, and he looked good.

The proper thing for me to do would have been to invite him in, but I chose not to. On the other hand, he could have attempted to come to the door to escort me to the car, but he didn't. I believe it was because of my preaching dad.

As I opened the car door, he said, "Happy Birthday." Then he handed me a card.

It said, *To a special lady in my life, May all your dreams come true on this very special day. Happy Birthday!*

With gratitude, I said, "Thank you Bill." I was feeling special already and wondered what the rest of the night would hold.

We went out of town to keep Karen from seeing me in her car. While he was driving, I noticed the gas needle was just about on empty.

"Bill, you need to stop at the gasoline station. You're just about on E."

"Hey, don't worry bout nothin'. I got it." I didn't know why, but he seemed to have a smirk on his face after making that statement.

Shortly after, we pulled up in front of an old rundown building. A sign on the front door revealed the name, "Goldie's Restaurant." Bill took me inside. There was no one available to seat us, so we sat down at the counter. The menus were already there. I noticed right away that the prices were a little high and wondered if Bill could afford it. He chose the buffet for us because it was less expensive.

As I walked up to fix my plate, the appearance of the food did not look too appealing. I wondered if Bill felt the same way. Putting something on my plate kept me from seeming ungrateful. I went to my seat, blessed the food, and began to eat.

I didn't care for the food at all. The tough roast beef, the dry rigatoni, and the unseasoned chicken soon had a napkin placed over it. The corn and the chicken noodle soup were okay. The vegetables on the salad bar needed to be refreshed. Personally, I would have preferred dining at "Bigmomma's Place." Bill pretended to enjoy the food. However, he didn't go up for seconds.

When it was time to pay the check, Bill scratched his head as if to be thinking. Then he said, "Hey girl, my cash is tied up a minute. You mind lending a helpin' hand? I'll pay you back later."

He had a lot of nerve. Too bad I had to pay for something I did not enjoy. I only hoped he would never bring me back here again.

"Sure," was all I could say. That's what I get for not telling him where I wanted to go for my birthday in the first place. The bill was paid, and we got up and left. Afterwards, he headed straight for the gasoline station and looked over at me. I pulled out another ten dollars from my purse.

Our next stop was on the other side of town at the "Club House." When we pulled up, cars were everywhere. It must have been a popular place to be. As we went in, we realized this must be "disco night." The man at the door collected one dollar from every person. As I reached in my purse, Bill took two dollars out of his pocket and paid the cover charge. There were wall-to-wall people.

Bill led me to a seat at the bar. It took about ten minutes for the bartender to wait on us. They were very busy. Bill ordered me a rum and coke and ordered himself vodka on the rocks. He pulled his wallet out and paid for the drinks.

I watched Bill order several drinks. It wasn't long before I blurted out, "Bill, please don't drink too much tonight. You know, you have to drive us home."

Bill looked at me strangely so I refrained from pushing the issue. Upsetting him was the last thing I wanted to do. The night had really just begun. It was my birthday, and I had every intention on enjoying it to the fullest.

"Sarah, lay off me. Don't need you tellin' me how much to drink. Let me handle mine. Now, I'm tryin' to show you a nice time, so chill out!"

The tone of his voice warned me that the nature of the evening could change quickly. I nursed my drink while he downed several more vodka's on the rocks.

Bill broke the mood with a friendlier, yet commanding tone. "Come on, let's dance." He grabbed me before I could say no.

I tried to keep up but to no avail. I had no coordination at all. It was breathtaking. He was all over the floor while I danced in one spot. I had no idea what I was doing and furthermore, what he was doing so I started doing the "Monkey." Nevertheless, it was all in fun.

Bill chilled out on his drinking the rest of the night, and I had a great time. We joked, laughed, and danced until 11:45 p.m. We were ready to go, "but the night was still young." As we drove around, the breeze in the air could not have been better.

All of a sudden, Bill put his right turn signal on and pulled up to a motel. He had never mentioned that we were going there. I hoped he wouldn't put me on the spot to pay for the room, because I didn't have any more money on me. Bill left me in the car while he went inside to register. I wondered what the inside of this place would look like.

Upon his return, he had a key in his hand to room 112. As we opened the door, there was a fresh clean smell with a full-sized bed in the middle of the room. The gorgeous frame was made of oak wood. Surprisingly, the rest of the furniture was nice, including the large-sized bathroom. The whole atmosphere in itself was rather pleasant.

Bill turned the television on and didn't waste any time pulling out a bag of reefer from his pocket. I sat down waiting for him to take the lead in the conversation. Quietly, he took out some cigarette papers, rolled up three joints, and then lit the first one. It must have been so powerful, because when he blew out the smoke, he had to sit down. Afterwards, he offered it to me. I objected.

"No thanks! That drink I had at the bar was enough. I've only tried reefer a couple of times, and it made me feel stupid. I really don't care for it."

Bill leaned toward me, locking his brown eyes with mine, and profoundly said, "Look girl, it's your birthday. Loosen up a little. It ain't goin' hurt you to take a couple of puffs. What you scared of?"

"I'm not scared. I just don't like the way it makes me feel!"

"That's cause you aint doin' it right. Look here, watch me." He took another puff. He inhaled it, held his breath, and then exhaled.

Bill had a serious look on his face and said, "Now try it."

He purposely blew the smoke right in my face, which gave me a contact high. However, I still refused. Bill finished the first joint and lit the second. Then he started sweating and began taking his shirt and shoes off.

"Well, maybe I should just take you home, girl. You ain't no fun at all. There are women out there who'd love to be gettin' high wit me right now. If I knew you were such an odd ball, I wouldn't have wasted my cash on you. We coulda' stayed at the bar and just had a couple drinks."

His tone began to change a notch. "I bought you here to show you a good time for your birthday, and now you just goin' disc me?"

The red circling around his irises seemed to be turning into an angry red, rather than the mellow scarlet that one would expect from smoking reefer. I wished upon seeing those mesmerized eyes or hoped he would put his shades back on. He leaned into me as if to ignite a feeling of power. "I ain't the one to play no games wit, Sarah!"

With an apologetic tone, I timidly said, "I'm sorry, Bill. I'll try it, but just a little." I didn't want to make him any angrier.

"My girl," Bill said, as he handed me the joint. Halfheartedly, I took one puff, then another, and then an additional puff not realizing the strength of it all. A minute later, I felt giggly. Bill sat there staring at me. Then he chuckled and said, "You okay?"

I smiled and nodded. I was so high, yet fully aware of my surroundings. Bill immediately took a little black case out of the pocket of his jacket and headed toward the bathroom. He didn't come out for what seemed like an hour. Whatever he was doing in there, made his eyes glassy, and the side of his mouth twitch. Something was not right.

Speaking softly, I said, "You okay?"

He never responded. The next thing I knew, he was pulling me onto the bed. He kissed my lips, almost roughly, while tugging on my shirt. I showed no resistance to his yearnings. Before I knew it, we were making passionate love and nothing else mattered.

CHAPTER SIX

THE WEEKS AND MONTHS SEEMED TO COME and go. I overlooked Bill's shortcomings, not realizing the destructive path that awaited me. I embraced the fact of wanting to be with Bill more than ever. Sometimes, he appeared to be glad to see me, and other times he seemed irritable, cold hearted, and distant.

One night I ran into him at the "Riverview Bar." He glared at me as if annoyed by my presence.

"Hi, Bill. I haven't heard from you in a while. I was beginning to worry."

Bill gave me the dirtiest look. He pushed his index finger towards my face. "I'm only goin' say this once, and you betta' get it straight. Don't come lookin' for me. If I wanna see you, I know where you at. You feel me?"

He spoke so loud that everyone turned around in bewilderment. I was startled but remained calm.

"Okay!" Someone must have gotten under his skin or maybe he lost money gambling. Normally, I would let things like this go; however, when the music started playing again, I apologized.

"I'm sorry. I was just concerned and didn't know if something happened or if you were with another woman."

Bill snapped again. "Another woman! Well, you knew that when you met me. Look girl; let's get something straight right now. I'm gonna be wit whoever I wanna be wit and when I wanna be wit them. If you don't like it, then stay the hell away from me!" He walked away and left me standing right in the middle of the bar. I "played it off" and went outside hoping he would come outside and apologize. His rudeness was unnecessary, so I headed home not quite understanding the nature of his actions. I felt empty inside and began to cry.

Bill became more and more disrespectful towards me as time went on. No man had ever treated me in this manner. The relationship was beginning to be a struggle. I hoped for better days, yet willing to give him the benefit of the doubt.

Six months had come and gone. The relationship showed no change for the better. It was obvious that Bill could be with one to five different women whenever he wanted to. When I would come around, he sometimes acted as if I didn't exist. Questioning Bill while he was with another female, resulted in embarrassment, so most of the time I said absolutely nothing. I went home many times hurt and humiliated.

One day, Bill called me on the phone. "Hey, just called to tell you that Karen's gettin' booted out cause she ain't paid her rent. She's movin' away from here. Looks like I gotta go wit her cause I ain't got nowhere else to stay."

I paused for a moment and started to slam the phone in his ear. The statements he previously made about being with other women hurt me tremendously. However, forgiving him was always in my heart.

I said, "Why don't you look for a room or an efficiency apartment? It won't cost that much. If you want me to, I can help you find one."

This seemed like a once in a lifetime opportunity to get him away from Karen. I decided to take advantage of it. I begged him not to go, and finally, he agreed that if I would help him find a room, he would not leave with Karen.

I was puzzled, though, about her not paying the rent because of her father's assistance. Nevertheless, it was none of my business.

The next day, we walked for hours trying to find Bill an affordable room or efficiency apartment. He complained the whole time. According to him, the first place was too close to the church. The second place was walking distance to my parents' house and neither one of us wanted that. He heard through other reliable sources that the third place had roaches. The fourth place had nosy neighbors. We looked at so many different available places. Picky Bill gave me excuse after excuse. I was tired of walking and became frustrated while trying not to lose my composure.

We finally took a rest and stopped by the store to get something to drink. I was so thirsty. By the end of the day, we finally found something that Bill agreed to take.

"Tijuana's Bar" had an efficiency apartment on the other side of the saloon. The owner, which we already knew, kindly showed us the place. The furnished room consisted of a bed, table, sink, stove, and refrigerator. The only thing unlikeable was the location of the bathroom, which was at the other end of the hallway. The tenants in the building had to share the same restroom.

The rent was $180 a month with utilities included. Bill reached into his pocket and pulled out his wallet, which had no money in it. He looked puzzled and said someone must have stolen his "doe." Out of desperation to keep him in town, I paid his first month's rent. The property owner gave him the keys. I was surprised they didn't do a background check.

I took off from work and offered to help clean his room before he moved anything in. The next day, we went to the store and bought some cleaning supplies. As soon as we got back to the room, I filled a bucket with an all-purpose cleaner, put on some rubber gloves, and thoroughly cleaned the furniture and appliances. Next, I got some clean water, used a disinfectant, and wiped down the mattress. Then I got on my hands and knees, and scrubbed the floor. Bill sat there relaxing and playing solitaire without a care in the world.

After a while, Bill started getting fidgety and ran in and out of the apartment. I ignored his mood change and continued to clean. Last, I took the bedclothes that were in a basket and went to the laundry mat. I was so exhausted. It took three days to get everything situated, and then Bill moved in.

Two weeks later, he allowed me to come back for a visit. Bill had a stereo, television, pictures to hang on his walls, new sheets and blankets, etc. He told me that Karen had given him some things. I dared not say anything for fear of an argument, but had that look on my face. Bill seemed to have read my mind.

"I hope you not thinkin' just cause you helped me out, you can rule my life. I ain't changed, and whatever my friends wanna do for me is none of your business."

I quietly sat there feeling like a complete idiot. I wasn't trying to rule his life; I just wanted to help.

Bill continued with his sarcasm. "I'm tellin' you now; don't ever fall in love wit me if you don't wanna get hurt. I ain't ready to settle down and stop comin' down here checkin' up on me."

Those statements pierced me right through my heart. I didn't want to hear any more and walked out the door. Bill jumped up and slammed the door.

Walking up the steep hill took forever as I headed home. It had begun to drizzle, but I didn't care. The rain would wash my tears away while listening to the wind and looking up at the sky.

After arriving at home, I sat on the porch for a few minutes trying to pull myself together prior to going in. There was no need for my family to know that something was bothering me. After going in and settling down, I spoke with my dad about the job and the supervisor position offered to me.

"Dad, I turned it down because it would have been too much responsibility."

"I don't blame you," dad said. "I'm surprised you lasted this long." He was familiar with the hard labor of working on the batteries.

I changed the conversation and asked dad if they heard from my oldest sister, Marie. She had been married and moved to California about a year ago. The last time we talked on the phone, she informed me about her pursuing a career in modeling. The whole family missed her terribly and wished she'd come back. Since she left, for some apparent reason, it has been so difficult to reach her.

Prior to her moving from Bentley Projects, I would visit her just to get away. Her apartment was by the basketball court where all the guys hung out. After her first marriage failed, she met a man who swept her off her feet. They both relocated to California where they soon eloped. Her new man treated her like a queen and called her Princess. In spite of the problems in her second marriage, she loved him for better or for worse. He was her Boaz. Her favorite and most common saying was *You know what.*

Marie was just downright silly and loud. Everything seemed to be so funny. One such example was when I purchased a beautiful sequence dress from the second hand store. It was gorgeous. In spite of the dress being three times smaller than my normal size, I was determined to squeeze in that no-button, no zipper dress. Unfortunately, it became very uncomfortable, so I decided to take it off. I pulled and tugged but was unsuccessful.

I called Marie on the phone and begged her to help me pull that dress off, but she was busy at the time. She didn't arrive at my house until three hours later. She "cracked up" laughing while her efforts failed to pull the dress over my head. I felt claustrophobic as the dress scraped my arms. I didn't find it funny at all. At any cost, that dress had to come off so I gave her scissors. Marie laughed hysterically the whole time while cutting the dress off me. She teased me for months.

Dad said they had heard from Marie about a couple of weeks ago and she seemed to be ok. I was glad to hear that.

After watching thirty minutes of television, I went into the kitchen and fixed Tina and me a bowl of homemade French vanilla ice cream. It was so good. Afterwards, we headed to bed. I was extremely exhausted.

Bill didn't call for a while and getting him off my mind wasn't easy. Every time I went to work, I found myself glancing up at his apartment building. There were times that I could have sworn that a female was looking out the window. The thought of another woman sleeping with him, made me sick to my stomach.

Finally, I gave in and began making excuses to come and see him. I would cook dinner and offer to bring him a plate. Sometimes, Bill would let me in if he didn't have company. If not, I would just go home, but unable to sleep from wondering what he was doing. No matter how bad he treated me, he could easily charm his way back into my life whenever he wanted to. If he needed a favor, he knew he could count on me.

One night, Bill called me on the phone. "I know it's late but can you stop by my crib tomorrow on your way home from work. I need to talk to you, "babe."

"What about? Is anything wrong?"

"No, just need to discuss sometin' wit you in person. See you round 4:00."

"All right," I said. Then he hung up. I began wondering what he could possibly have to talk to me about. Maybe he would tell me not to come around anymore because he was in a serious relationship with someone else. All kind of thoughts went through my mind.

However, he must have been in a good mood because he called me, "babe." Racking my brain did not help matters. That night I went to bed early without knowing what to expect the following day because of unpredictable Bill.

CHAPTER SEVEN

"WHAT YOUR MOM CHARGE YOU FOR RENT?" Bill asked.

"Why did you ask me that?" I wondered where this was leading.

"Just answer me!"

"Around $200.00 a month. Is there a problem?"

Before he could answer me, there was a sudden knock on the door. Bill opened it. It was Jerry Caldwell, a major drug dealer. I wondered what he could possibly want with Bill. As far as I knew, they were never friends, just casual acquaintances.

"Yo man, what up?" Bill greeted him, slapping him five. "Perfect timing. Sarah was just leavin'." Bill put his arm around me and pulled me out of the room.

As he walked me to the door, Bill said, "We can talk about this some more later. Meet me on the hill round seven. Later, 'babe.'"

My mind suddenly went back to the pocketful of money Bill had when we went to "Bigmomma's Place" for lunch. Then, I thought about the black bag at the hotel room. A certain feeling came over me while on my way out the door.

As I got closer to the top of the hill, a horn blew. I looked around and saw that it was Bobby. He offered me a ride home. I gladly accepted.

"Hey, Bobby, I haven't seen you in ages. Where have you been?"

"I went to Philly to visit my Pops, got back home yesterday."

"Well, how is he?"

"The ole man is fine. What about you?"

"Oh, I'm fine. I had to work today, so I'm on my way home."

"It is nice to see you again," said Bobby. "You think maybe we could get together later on?"

"I don't think so. I'm seeing someone else now, but thanks for the ride," I said while getting out the car. Bobby grunted, blew the horn, and pulled off.

There was two hours to kill before meeting Bill again. As I walked into the house, the aroma of dinner smelled all over the place. Mom made spaghetti/meatballs with toss salad and garlic bread. I washed my hands and immediately fixed my plate. The dinner was scrumptious. After supper, I did my chores and then took a shower.

The temperature would be in the mid to upper 70's that evening, so I put on my blue jean shorts, a sleeveless tank top, and my white sneakers. After putting my hair in a ponytail, I headed down the street.

I spotted Bill right away. He was standing alone, but there were quite a few people on the other side of the street. The closer we got to each other, the more visible the bouquet of flowers became that was in his hand. I wondered if they were for me. It's not very often that I receive flowers.

Bill embraced me and handed me the beautiful flowers. I began to look around to see if anyone was observing my reaction. To my knowledge, they wasn't.

"What's this for?" I wondered what I had done to deserve this kind of treatment.

"This is for the special lady you are. You are no doubt, my queen."

I was flabbergasted. No man had ever said those words to me. Then, he put his arm around me and we walked across the street.

"The banana split is on me, 'babe.'" We went into Julia's ice cream parlor, sat at a booth, and Bill ordered us a small vanilla ice cream cone. I enjoyed the moment and didn't want the evening to end.

"Hey 'babe.'" Do you remember what we were talkin' bout earlier?" Bill held my hands up to his.

"Do you mean about the rent that I pay my mom?"

He nodded.

"What about it?"

"Well, I was thinkin', we have been seein' each other bout six months or so. Right?"

"I believe so." My eyes began to light up.

"Forgive me for failin' to show it, but I really do care bout you. Ever since I met you, all my homies been tellin' me you are a good woman, and I need to stop actin' up and settle down wit you. You always been here for me. I don't wanna lose you, 'babe.'"

"Oh don't be silly," I blushed. "You are not going to lose me." This was the first time that he opened up to me about what people were saying and how he felt.

Bill continued, "Need to ask you a very important question."

I had never seen Bill look so serious. He gave me eye contact, but I glanced away. It was still very difficult for me to give Bill or anyone eye contact for more than a couple of seconds at a time.

"Go ahead. I'm listening."

"Instead of payin' yo mom $200.00 a month for rent, why don't you move in wit me? We could chill here for a little while, save some money, and then move into a bigger apartment or, better yet, a house. How you feel bout that, Sarah? You wit me? Tina can sleep on the couch and we can sleep in the bed."

He looked at me with the sweetest brown eyes that one could imagine and waited patiently for me to answer. I was bewildered. "Of course I'd like that, but if you don't mind, I have one question that I'd like to ask you."

"Speak about it, 'babe.'"

"When did you decide all of this and why now?" I was curious and had to know.

"That was two questions, but I'll answer them truthful as possible. Been thinkin' bout this for the last couple months. The reason I ain't asked you before was cause you wasn't ready for me. I believe we gotta better understandin' now. You know how I am and I know how you are. You know what I'm sayin'?"

Living with him had been in the back of my mind for quite a while. I was too afraid to mention it for fear of rejection. I thought it was out of the question.

"What would you expect of me, Bill?" I wanted to know what my obligations and responsibilities would be.

"All I want is for you to love me," Bill claimed.

Well, that sounded easy enough for me. The feelings were already there. "I need a few days to break it down to my parents." Bill didn't need to know that it would be a big problem with them.

Sarcastically, Bill said, "The last I knew, you were a grown woman. Take your time, but hurry up for I change my mind."

I looked at him and smiled. I was delighted that he finally asked me. Bill paid for my ice cream, and then he walked me half way home.

I wasn't exactly sure what to say to my parents, but figured there would be some drama. They can't run my life anymore, and I deserve to be happy. My sister, Marie, lived with a man before she got married so why can't I? They were going to have to accept it whether they like it or not. I will courageously confront them tomorrow.

However, when the big announcement day came, the courage vanished. I was so nervous about getting into a confrontation that I decided to go at it in a different approach. The next night, I deliberately kept Tina home with me, and waited for my parents to go to church. It would be two hours before they would be back home, which gave me an opportunity to pack our clothes quickly. I had no other choice but to leave some things behind. The clock was ticking.

I started to panic because Bill had not called. He was supposed to pick us up no later than 9:00 p.m. Finally, at 9:45, he blew the horn. We were gone by 10 p.m., after quickly grabbing our clothes, my television, and a few miscellaneous items including some of Tina's toys.

Tina asked, "Where we goin', Mommy? Why are we takin' all dis stuff?"

I grabbed her hand and said, "We will talk about it later."

Leaving a note would have been the proper thing for me to do. However, I was so busy rushing to get out of the house that it didn't cross my mind at the time. This ordeal wasn't planned very well at all, nor the thought of facing the consequences. I should have thought things through before accepting the invitation.

I had to go back to work within two days, and now needed a reliable babysitter. I was not the type of mother to let anyone watch my child, so it wasn't easy finding the right person. A friend at work recommended her neighbor, Miss Josephine Patterson.

Miss Patterson was a sweet, little 72-year-old nosy woman who lived in the projects. I thought she was a little too old to babysit, but didn't have much choice on such short notice. She charged me five dollars a day. I offered to pay her more. At first, she seemed glad to be helping. Later, I realized it wasn't such a good idea, after all.

At the end of the workweek, I went to pick up Tina. When I arrived at Miss Patterson's house, she opened the door with tears in her eyes. "Tina is not here. Your mother came by to pick her up. I am so, so, sorry."

A part of me wanted to get upset with Miss Patterson for allowing my mother to take Tina. On the other hand, I couldn't because she had been so sweet and kind. Without asking any questions, I put my arms around her and told her that everything would be okay. I thanked her for her time and gave her fifty dollars for the week and left.

Immediately, I stormed to a pay phone and called my mother. She had the nerve to take my daughter behind my back without my permission. "Hello Mother," I scowled. "Why did you come and take Tina?"

"Because I'm not going to have Tina living under those conditions!"

I was angry. "What do you mean? Tina was being well taken care of!"

Mom started screaming at me. "Did you think that I wouldn't find out where you were living at? I will not allow Tina to be exposed to such an environment! We raised you better than that!"

I screamed back. "Well, it's my life, and she's my daughter, and I want her back!" I was so upset I started crying.

Mom didn't care. She said, "I can't do anything about what you do with your life, but you will not get Tina back until you find a place of your own, and Tina has her own bedroom." Then she hung up on me.

I picked up the phone and called her back but to no avail. She wouldn't answer the phone. I knew better than to go up there with my dad home. He would have knocked me down. Mom and dad "did not play that."

I sat down on the curb by the payphone crying while trying to think things through. Too much was happening.

While walking down the hill to Bill's room feeling emotionally torn, it felt like a part of my life was gone. I didn't know what to do. My parents didn't seem to understand. Taking them to court would have been the logical thing to do, but I didn't want to put Tina through those procedures. In addition, the possibility dawned on me that the court might agree with my parents.

When I got back to the room, Bill was fumbling with a padlock on the outside of the door. I was too emotionally exhausted to question him.

CHAPTER EIGHT

THE FIRST TWO WEEKS I STAYED WITH BILL, he was as nice as one could be. He made breakfast for us, and at night, we would cuddle up and watch a movie.

Bill said, "You get your pay tomorrow, right?"

I paused for a second. "Yes, I do. Why? What's up?"

"I'm runnin' short of cash, and need $150.00 till next week. Got somethin' I need to take care of."

I was starting to learn Bill and knew deep down in my heart, he would not pay me back. My check would be $500.00. The next day I gave him the money before going to see about the rent. To my surprise, Bill hadn't paid rent in two months. Therefore, payment in the amount of $160.00 and a $20.00 late fee was due or else he would be getting an eviction notice. That left me with a total of $170.00, which was just enough to buy food and miscellaneous items for the next two weeks.

Buying all the food was no problem. Bill said this was my obligation no matter what other expenses occurred. I wanted so much to be a good woman, and tried not to complain. However, the expectation to loan him money before finding out that he was two months behind in his rent didn't set very well with me. Yet, I kept my mouth shut.

It was necessary to budget the rest of my paycheck. I went to the grocery store and purchased mostly store brand products or items that were on sale. My mother taught me to stock up on coupons, which came in handy.

While putting away the food, I felt great. Now I could see Bill nightly since we were a true couple.

I meticulously cooked a very nice dinner for Bill. The dinner consisted of sirloin steak with green peppers and mushrooms. The steak complemented the twice-baked potato topped with butter, shredded cheese, and bacon bits. My choice for fried cabbage and homemade cornbread completed the meal. While everything was cooking, I made a pitcher of freshly squeezed lemonade. There was more than enough food in case any of Bill's friends stopped by.

Dinner was done around 6:30 p.m. I was so sure that Bill would be here by now. The table was set with a very lavishly laced tablecloth purchased for special occasions. I didn't use the new dishes and wine glasses because of not wanting to wash them. I was so hungry, but wanted to wait on Bill before fixing my plate. The candlelight dinner was ready. I turned down the oven temperature to keep the food warm.

Every time a car door closed, I would jump up and peek out the window, only to be disappointed. The clock ticked away and the time was now 8 p.m. In a couple of hours, it would be time for me to get ready to work my scheduled-midnight shift. I needed to get a couple hours of sleep, but instead, sat there disillusioned and lost my appetite. At 9:30 p.m., I put the food away. My plans had been to surprise Bill, but the surprise was solely on me.

My worn-out body made it difficult to work the whole night without falling asleep. In spite of how I felt, I managed to do my job efficiently. On my breaks, drinking coffee along with eating several chocolate candy bars helped me tremendously.

When arriving home the next morning, I expected Bill to be sleeping. He was not. By appearance of the room, he had not been there all night. No sooner after lying down and closing my eyes, Bill came in the door. His eyes were as red as fire and his mouth twitched. I was too tired to argue or question him, and tried not to let my thoughts get the best of me.

I just said, "Good morning, Bill!" The room began to smell like a brewery.

Bill ignored me, which made me sit straight up in the bed. "How was your night, Honey? I was a little worried when I came home and you weren't here."

Bill still didn't respond and started pacing the floor and going through his dresser as if looking for something. I tried my best to stay calm. "I fixed dinner for you yesterday and made your favorite dish, T-bone steak, but you never came home."

Before I could say anything else, Bill snapped. "Are you questionin' me? This is my house, and I do what I please! If you don't like it, there's the door!"

His unexpected behavior baffled me. Just the other day he was so loving and kind. "I'm sorry, I didn't mean any harm. Can I get you a cup of coffee or fix you a nice hot breakfast?"

"No thanks!" Bill roared. Then he took a change of clothes and stormed angrily out the door.

I sat for a moment stunned, but was too exhausted to ponder on his actions and remarks. I lay back down and didn't wake up until 3 p.m.

I woke up thinking about Tina. She would often nudge me while I was asleep. Boy was she missed. The time will eventually come for me to have my own place and then I will get her back. At least she was okay.

For the next week and a half, Bill was in and out of the apartment. I rarely saw him, but continued to keep his room clean and cooked regardless of the tiredness in my body from working. I concealed the fact of feeling like a recipient of his heartless and dual emotions.

One particular day, while on my hands and knees scrubbing the carpet, Bill walked in. He took his shoes and hat off. "Why you on the floor?"

"There's some mud prints on the floor, and I was trying to get it up before you came home."

He lifted me off the floor and said, "Don't worry bout it, 'babe.' Clean that mess up some other time." Then he held me in his arms and told me how much he missed me.

To my astonishment, he stayed in with me the rest of the day. He was in a good mood. "Hey, 'babe.' There's a softball game at the ball field. Heard it starts at 6 p.m. Wanna go?"

I smiled and said, "Sure, but let me cook dinner first."

His demeanor struck me by surprised, but I did not intend to question it. We had plenty of time before the game started, so I took a pack of pork chops out of the freezer and quickly thawed it under cold running water. Bill looked in the cupboard and took out a box of garlic roasted-flavored mashed potatoes, which he fixed in no time. Then, he looked in the refrigerator and saw enough fresh vegetables to make a scrumptious tossed salad.

"Honey, you ain't had a salad till you tried mine. May I have the honor?" He kissed my hand.

"Be my guest." While he was making the salad, I fried the pork chops. You would have thought we were the happiest couple in the world. Finally, I would get a chance to use the lavishly laced-tablecloth again and the sparkling crème colored dishes.

Bill found a vanilla-scented candle from the cupboard, placed it in the middle of the table, and lit it. We both sat down, and I blessed the food.

"Lord, we thank you for this meal. Bless those that have and bless those that have not. Let it be nourishment to our bodies. Amen."

We didn't have any wine, so Bill poured soda into our lustrous-gold glasses and held his up to make a toast:
"To the sweetest lady in the world."

After dinner, Bill helped me clean up for a change. He scraped the dishes, and I washed them. It surely felt good to see Bill act like a perfect gentleman. I didn't want to concern myself about how long this would last. It just behooved me, to just, enjoy the moment.

We finished the dishes and put the food away. I grabbed a change of clothes and went down the hall to take a shower. While meditating on the romantic day, all of a sudden, reality hit me. *How could I be so dumb?*

Bill's niceness, most likely, was because of my payday in a couple more days. I should have known. While getting dressed, I decided to keep my feelings to myself for fear of an intense argument. Today was such an extraordinary and wonderful day with him. Exposing the truth of the whole matter would definitely spoil it.

Besides, I loved him and was hopeful for his returned love one day, if only I could be patient enough to wait.

While Bill took his shower, I ironed his jeans and shirt. Ironing was one of my least favorite tasks. After he got dressed, we walked to the softball field. Our team, the "77's," played against the "Field Raiders."

We stopped at the concession stand and Bill bought the popcorn. While the game went on, he threw popcorn in the air and caught it in his mouth. He acted very silly, and I loved every moment of it.

Every time the "77's" would score, Bill would jump up and yell, "All right!" He certainly was a fan.

The game was almost over with the "77's" in the lead. As I looked around the crowd, my eyes unexpectedly met the eyes of Miss Josephine Patterson, my former babysitter. Halfheartedly, I waved and quickly turned my head. Her reputation was still one of being the nice little old woman who knew everybody's business.

The game was over, but Bill was still yelling over the victory. After seeing the likes of Miss Patterson, I began to get a little embarrassed. Leading Bill by the hand in the opposite direction was to no avail. Before I knew it, someone tapped me on the shoulder. I turned around, as if surprised.

"Oh, hi Miss Patterson, it's so nice to see you again. I didn't know you were a fan of the "77's" softball team. Didn't they play a good game today?"

"They played an outstanding game. I try my best to come to most of their home games because my grandson plays on the team. Did you see all the homeruns he almost made?"

"I saw him," I mumbled, not really knowing which one was her grandson. "Well, you have a nice day."

I tried my best to walk away while Bill chatted with one of his friends. Miss Patterson kept walking right behind me. The faster I walked, the faster she walked. Clearly, I recognized she was not as slow and feeble as she pretended to be. She strutted as if a miracle in her body just took place. She walked faster than her grandson ran trying to make a home run.

Miss Patterson was persistent. "Oh, by the way, how's Tina?" Before I could turn around and answer, she stepped on the back of my heel, and knocked my right tennis shoe off my foot. I was fuming. She scraped a little skin off my heel too, and it started burning.

"She's fine!" I hissed, while trying to keep my composure after being irritated.

"Well, tell her I said hello, and to come and see me sometime." Miss Patterson laughed. She knew she knocked my shoe off and didn't even bother to say sorry or excuse me. I thought that was so rude.

"I'll do that." I didn't want to give her nosy self a chance to ask me anything else. Fortunately, someone else caught her attention, which gave me an outlet to escape and find Bill. I put my shoe back on and then we headed towards home.

When we were one block from home, Bill said, "Let's race. Bet I beat you home."

"I bet you can't."

Bill said, "And if I win, what I get?"

I put my finger on my cheek, and said, "Well, let me see. If you win, I'll invite Miss Patterson over for dinner. If I win, you have to take Miss Patterson out for dinner to a nice restaurant without me." Before I could finish my sentence, Bill took off running.

"That is not fair," I said, while vigorously running behind him. "You cheated. The bet's off." We laughed and laughed.

After we arrived at home, I said, "Bill, I had such a nice time with you today. You are so crazy."

I cut the television on, and we sat on the love seat that someone had given Bill.

Bill turned the TV off and said, "Let's talk!" I had no idea what he wanted to talk about this time, so I just sat there waiting for him to start the conversation.

"Sarah, we been seein' each other for a while now. You say you love me and I believe you do." I listened attentively.

Bill continued. "Had a good time today, walking. That was all-good, but, I would like to take my lady out in a car, my own car. Then I can take you food shoppin' and everywhere else you need to go. Now that would really make me happy."

My response was quick. "Well, what did you have in mind?"

61

Linda Foster

"Just somethin' decent to get round in. Saw a 1965 Oldsmobile for sale cross the street from the post office. The price was only 400 bucks. I took it for a test drive and it drives pretty well. I have half the money and need you to come up wit the other two hundred bucks. You wit me? One more thing, I need you to put the car in your name."

Bill watched closely for my reaction. The price was very affordable, and it seemed like it would benefit the both of us. At least there would not be any monthly payments to make. We did need our own transportation especially to go to the Laundromat and shopping. Besides, not having to catch the bus would give me more time to do things with Tina. It would also be to my advantage to put the vehicle in my name, just in case the relationship didn't work out.

CHAPTER NINE

WITHIN A MONTH AND A HALF, I saved enough money to help buy our first car, a tan Oldsmobile. Surprisingly, it was still sitting; nobody had bought it. He previously told me the price was $400.00. Either he lied or the price went up. It was $600.00 plus tax. Bill paid the $200.00 that he agreed on, and I had to pay the rest.

The fifteen-year-old Oldsmobile was a two door, with gray vinyl seats. I'm glad it had an AM/FM radio. It was very clean. This particular vehicle had only one owner, who took very good care of it. We were excited after the purchase.

For the most part, Bill took me where I needed to go. We had it for five months until Lucy Cambridge ran into our parked vehicle, and totaled it. No one was hurt. Luckily, Bill was at the scene of the accident when it happened. She gave him her information along with her telephone number. Bill immediately took down her license plate number.

After getting several estimates, we quickly got in touch with her and sent the highest one, which was $900.00. She didn't have car insurance, so she came up with the cash. I didn't understand why she gave the money to Bill. She was well aware that the car was in my name.

Instead of getting the car fixed or buying another one, Bill blew it on drugs and gambling. He would come home so blasted. It was evident that he had been doing something more than smoking reefer.

"Bill, you're high, aren't you? Where's the money for the car?"

I was so disgusted at him.

Bill got in my face. "Yeah, I ain't feelin' no pain. What about it? It's all yo fault anyway. Got somethin' you wanna say? If not, your best bet is to get out of my face!"

I didn't respond and Bill never admitted to blowing the money. However, it was obvious. I just looked at him with a frown on my face, unable to get over the fact that he actually blamed me. It would be useless to quarrel with him, so I ignored him for the rest of the evening.

Weeks and months went by and no matter what he did, I felt giving up on him was not the solution. Things will change--they had to. I loved him for better or worse. That love was unconditional.

Eventually, Bill had a new conversation with me about buying another vehicle. "Hey 'babe.'" I'm gettin' tired of walkin' and payin' jitneys to take me places. How bout us getting a van? I'm talkin' bout some hard earned cash made by movin' people."

I was hesitant at first, but gave in to his desires. "Sounds like an honest job to me. The only thing, I don't know how to drive a van."

"Nothin' to it, Honey. You drive it, just like a car, only you gotta use the side mirrors to see what's beside you." Bill made it sound so easy.

There were other things to consider. Neither one of us had the money. It would take years to save up enough to buy a van in mint condition unless I went to the credit union and took out a loan.

That's exactly what Bill persuaded me to do.

Two weeks later, after completing the paper work, I purchased a 1975 Chevy Van. It was off-white highlighted with a brown strip on both sides. The AM-FM radio/cassette player had a nice sound system. The plush-brown carpet complemented the bed in the back that folded into a seat. The mileage wasn't bad and the van had just passed inspection. It was perfect for us. The only disadvantage was that it had no power steering. The wheel was very hard to turn. Bill had planned to get that fixed. Unfortunately, it was not a front-wheel drive either, but that was ok.

My payments were $275.00 per month. I could afford this as long as there was no unnecessary spending.

Bill taught me how to drive the van. For the most part, it wasn't as hard as I thought. Getting used to parking while paying attention to the side mirrors, would take a little practice.

After the excitement wore off, Bill resumed back to his old ways. We got into many arguments about the van. He seemed to have taken complete control over it. He rarely picked me up from work and was not around when I needed to go somewhere. When it was my payday, he always seemed to surface.

I found myself constantly questioning Bill. "Why didn't you pick me up from work? I was tired and here I had to walk up the hill to go to the store. Not only that, I had to carry those heavy bags all the way back down the hill." I was upset. Sometimes it was the Laundromat as well as other places that I needed to go.

His arrogant reply was, "I was busy. The walk ain't killed you, did it? Good exercise for you!"

I also depended on him to take me to my doctor's appointment. My birth control pills mysteriously disappeared, and I needed more. Rescheduling appointments took place numerous times because Bill never seemed to have the time to take me. He made excuse after excuse. Catching up with him seemed next to impossible, especially when I needed him the most. If I did, many times he had another woman in the van.

To save myself from the embarrassment, I had to humble myself and say calmly, "I need to go to the store. Can you please take me when you get time?"

"Well, you just gotta wait," he said with hostility.

For some reason, everyone seemed to come before me, and it just wasn't right.

The relationship took a toll on me. On some occasions, I was unwilling to give him the funds that he asked for. When that happened, he seemed compelled to take it. Because of his cruel actions, I began hiding my money. However, Bill found it the majority of the time.

An incident happened one night as I came into the apartment building. Before entering the premises, I decided to take the money out of my purse and hide it in one of my socks. Meanwhile, I was unaware that Bill had been sitting in someone's car and witnessed my so-called careful decision. Soon after my entrance into the room, he stormed in, slammed the door, and locked it. He grabbed me by my shirt and pulled me close. I was afraid!

Bill was in a rage. "Did I ever, ever, hide money from you?"

At first, I was unable to respond for fear of no matter what I said; it would be the wrong answer.

With his other hand, he slapped me in the face. "I'm goin' ask you this one more time! Did I ever hide money from you?"

Because of the unexpected situation, I knew it was to my best interest to respond immediately. "No."

I began to cry. My face felt a strike from the palm of his hand a second time. Then he pushed me. I fell to the floor.

"We supposed to be a team, Sarah. Don't be hidin' nothin' from me. I brought you here, thinkin' I could help you save some money. And look at your sorry self!" He lifted his leg and got ready to kick me. I doubled over, covered my head, and screamed.

"You know what, Sarah? You are just downright pitiful!"

I slowly got up and moved toward the door. Bill picked me up as if I was weightless and slammed me down on the floor. "We ain't done talkin' bout this!" He warned that it wasn't safe trying to run.

As he rummaged through my socks, he called me a dirty name--a name he had never called me before. Bill collected every folded bill that he found. I scooted away from him and leaned against the wall. My back was hurting from the knock down. I dared not stand.

While sobbing, I pulled my legs to my chest and cradled my head. After he took all the bills, he threw my socks at me. I was afraid to speak and afraid to move. He held the money in my face angrily but victoriously, and then placed it in his wallet. I was out of $200.00 that night and never got it back.

I wanted to leave and go home to my parents but was afraid because of his state of mind. Bill would take a while to calm down. When he did, he stated that even though I had broken his trust, he forgave me. He apologized for overreacting. Each time he sounded sincere.

My body was so sore.

This was just the beginning of the physical abuse that escalated in a matter of time. Each time, I thought that just possibly, this would be my last incident of abuse from Bill. He kept promising not to do it again.

Bill began constantly cussing at me and calling me names. It became a normal part of my life. "The very next time you come lookin' for me or accusin' me of bein' wit another woman, I'm goin' to....."

Sometimes, he would push me into the van, take me home, threaten me, and tell me I had better stay there. If he thought there was a possibility of my leaving, he sometimes would lock me in the apartment by putting a padlock on the outside of the door.

Now I realized that's why he bought that lock. Anytime it was in his hands, I rushed towards the door alongside of him.

"No!" I pleaded. "Please don't lock me in here. Please!"

Bill would push me in the room, run out the door, and lock it in spite of my pleading. "Shut up...!" He said.

By now, I was frantic. "Please don't do this to me! What if I have to go to the bathroom?"

"Well, tough luck," he yelled from the outside of the door. "Go in a cup or either go on yourself. I don't give a.... And you better not climb out the window either!"

The window was too small to be an option. Many times, he didn't return until morning.

I began to feel like a prisoner. Instead of things getting better, they got worse. Bill seemed to have a psychological hold on me, especially since I didn't know what I was doing wrong. The feeling of being in a box, unable to get out, created a feeling of despair.

My mom was right. Tina did not need to be in this type of environment. According to my parents, living with a man who is not your husband is a sin. However, I missed her tremendously and wanted to see my little girl.

I decided to swallow my pride and go to my parents' house once again. I told Bill I needed the van for a couple of hours to take Tina and some of her friends to a birthday party. I dropped him off at his cousin's house. I'm surprised he went for it. I went back to his room, packed my clothes quickly, and headed home to face the music.

CHAPTER TEN

I SAT IN MY VAN FOR A WHILE after pulling up to the house, waiting for the courage to knock on the door. Even though I still had my key, this would not be a good time to use it. Six months had gone by since my last conversation with them.

I rang the doorbell while waiting for someone to "chew me out." Mom opened the door. Before I could open my mouth to apologize, tears began streaming down her face. She welcomed me with the warmest smile you could ever imagine.

Dad looked at me, choked up, and said, "I've been praying for this day!"

I was in total awe and felt like the prodigal daughter coming back home. Tina, my baby girl, seemed like she grew a couple of inches. She ran and jumped in my arms.

"Mommy! Mommy! Mommy's home!"

With tears streaming down my face, I said, "Yes, baby, and I'm here to stay." I just wanted to hold her and never let go. While embracing her, I walked over to mom.

"Mom, I don't know what has gotten into me lately. I'm going through something right now and haven't been myself. I am so sorry for the way I reacted. I should have talked it over with you before I took Tina."

Mom seemed to feel my pain. "I just want the best for you and Tina. Don't ever feel that we are not here for you. We love you, and you can talk to us anytime you need to. We might not always agree with you, but we are concerned. It's a cruel world out there."

I looked at dad and said, "I'm sorry."

Dad had a serious look on his face. "Sarah, God is concerned about you. If he can forgive you, so can I, but you better not ever talk to your mother like that again!"

I thought he was through when all of a sudden, he said, "Let's have a word of prayer right now." He told us to make a circle and hold hands and then he prayed. We bowed our heads and closed our eyes.

Father God, we thank you. We thank you for this family and for bringing our daughter back home. Lord, we ask that you would do what needs to be done in her life. Stretch out your mighty hand and give her a mind to surrender. And Father God, we ask that you save all our children, and give us what to do when we don't know what to do, and we will give you all the glory and honor, and praise, for it all belong to you, in Jesus name, Amen.

The very moment he finished praying, mom started speaking in an unknown tongue. That language was similar to what I've heard in church as a young child. Out of respect, and not knowing what to do, I stood there speechless and just glanced at her every so often. I wondered why she wasn't speaking in English. Mom continued for about ten minutes straight.

While attentively listening, I learned a couple of words myself and thought that maybe I'd use it on Bill when he made me mad. After that ordeal was over, Tina came and gave me another hug. She seemed like she really missed me.

A week's vacation from my job was necessary just to recuperate emotionally. The prayer had done wonders for me. Spending quality time with Tina and my family was all I wanted. Tina and I went to the playground every day. She enjoyed swinging and sliding down the sliding board. This was an enjoyable moment.

At night, after putting her to bed, the cool breeze from the front porch was exceptionally relaxing. I sat on the porch swing for an hour and a half before going in.

I started going back to church and sensed an unexplainable peace. A month had gone by since last seeing Bill. He didn't look for me, and I didn't look for him--not even on my way to and from my job. However, I was hoping not to be tested.

One evening as I was leaving work, my job associate, Susan, approached me and handed me a letter. After arriving home, I finished my chores and then got Tina settled. Then I went to my room, closed the door, and read the letter:

Dear Sarah,

Hey, Babe! What's happenin'? Missin' you more and more every day. I know I messed up, but please hear me out. All my life, I've messed wit street woman, so that's what I'm used to. When I met you, you caught me by surprise. You have a good heart, you're caring, and I know you here for me. I done did a lot of things to you, and I said a lot of things about you. I'm sorry! Can't promise you the world, can't promise to change overnight, but if you give me half a chance, I promise to do better. Sarah, you the best thing that ever happened to me and I don't wanna lose you. Roses are red, violets are blue, sugar is sweet, but not as sweet as you are. Meet me at the crib tonight. I miss you.

Love,
Bill.

After reading that letter, it was hard not to think about Bill. My pacing the floor and trying to fight the feeling did not help matters. By 8 p.m., I found myself back down the "crib." He was waiting for me and seemed sincere when he looked me in the eyes and apologized repeatedly. Then he hugged and kissed me.

The subject came up about making our relationship work. I was hopeful. Staying that night was not an option, but within a few days, we were back together again.

The honeymoon didn't last long. Within a week, he was back to his same old self. Disappointment became a habitual part of my life. I was so sure the relationship would work this time. Now, I needed some answers as to why it didn't.

I said, "Why don't you stay home a little more, and why don't you like to take me out any more?" His response was not what I expected.

Bill took his hand, placed it under my chin, and made me look him square in the face. "You sure you wanna know the truth. Okay, I'll tell you. We ain't got nothin' in common. You don't get high. The little bit of weed you smoke don't mount to nothin', and you dance like you been taking lessons from a retired robot. Want some more?"

My voice began to crack as I held back the tears. "No thank you."

Bill continued anyway. "You don't know how to socialize wit other people when you out. All you do is sit there lookin' stupid, wit your glasses hangin' off your nose. You ain't nothin' but a square! And just look at how you dress. Your clothes look like they came from a rummage sale and most of them ain't fitting you right anyway. And that wig is just disgusting. All that hair you got and you wanna put on a wig. I'm sick and tired of lookin' at that mop you call a wig!"

Then he snatched the wig off my hair and threw it into the garbage. I let out a yell and grabbed my head. It hurt because of the numerous bobby pins holding the wig in place. Bill grabbed a mirror, squeezed my cheeks, and continued criticizing me.

"Take a good look in the mirror. Your pug nose adds to your ugliness. I always had pretty women round me. You the only one I ever had that's ugly. You messin' up my image. The only thing you got goin' on is your white teeth and your pretty smile. That's it, "Tackhead." Where he came from, "Tackhead" is what they call women who were no good. He pushed me onto the bed and left without retracting any of his comments.

Linda Foster

For about five minutes, I sat there on the side of the bed with my head down and both hands on my forehead. Next, I took the hand held mirror and held it up to my face. Bill was right about everything he said. I began to cry.

Labeling me as an ugly nobody emotionally damaged me. Going into bars was not on my agenda for a while. The only thing I did was go to the Laundromat, work, and shopping. I didn't want to be around anyone but my folks. They accepted me no matter what.

I never told anyone what he said to me. This hold Bill had on me was unexplainable. I should have left him then.

Bill never apologized for what he said. He continued running in and out and doing whatever he wanted to do including being with his ex girlfriend. She was from his hometown and decided to come and pay him a visit. Bill warned me just before her arrival.

"Deborah's comin' to town, and I don't want no mess out of you. She only stayin' a few days, and I'm gonna be with her, whether you like it or not. So, why don't you do yo-self a favor and go to your dear mother's till Deborah leaves."

I felt betrayed and spoke up without thinking or caring about possible consequences. "You must be out of your mind. I'm not going nowhere!" I was extremely tired of him "playing me."

Bill looked at me. Shockingly, he didn't force me to leave. He called me a "Tackhead" and walked away.

I went to work with an attitude and couldn't wait for my shift to end. Those eight hours seemed like sixteen. It had rained practically the whole shift. After getting back to the room, I found myself peeking out of the window often trying to catch a glimpse of Bill with someone.

After about an hour of looking attentively, there they were. I assumed the woman was Deborah. They were holding each other's arm going into the club. Bill was clean. He was dressed in a three-piece white suit with a cream-colored "super fly" hat that tilted to the side. He must have changed clothes while I worked my 3-11 second shift. Deborah had on a black and white pantsuit, with a white purse to match her shoes. I couldn't tell if her braided hair was a weave or not. The bright streetlights revealed all I needed to observe.

The club was in the next block from where we lived. No matter what happens, he is not going to get away with betraying me this time. I had enough and quickly changed clothes and went to face the culprit. I told someone to tell Bill to come outside for a moment. When he finally did, about fifteen minutes later, he was fuming and so was I.

Bill snared, "What .... do you want? Didn't I tell you not to spoil my night?"

I responded, "Why are you doing this to me? You are driving me insane! I love you! Why can't I get the respect that I deserve?"

With veins popping out of his forehead, Bill pointed his finger in my face. "You better leave me alone, if you got any sense!" He began gritting his teeth.

I started to walk away but was so full of rage that the palm of my hand accidently swung toward his face for the first time. He caught my hand while cussing me out. Next, he knocked me on the ground. My legs seemed to get out of control as Bill grabbed them. I mistakenly kicked him with my muddy shoes. In the midst of the tussling, his white suit got dirty, and his cream-colored hat fell off his head into a pile of mud. Mr. Clean wasn't clean anymore.

Bill was yelling like an ill-tempered lunatic. "Look what you did! I ought a kill you...! This is the first and last time you will ever put your hands on me. I'll deal wit you later!"

He went back into the bar and someone helped me from off the ground. I went back to the room sore and limping, yet satisfied for messing up his night.

Approximately ten minutes later, Bill brought Deborah to the room. I looked at her, and she looked at me up and down with a smirk on her face. She didn't speak.

"Is this your woman?" I was determined to put him on the spot, but hopeful that he didn't claim her.

"Yea, she been mine for two years, and I love my "Babe." What about it? I don't love you, never have, and never will. Now, you satisfied?"

I was always unsure of his love for me, but to actually tell me that to my face and in front of another woman just crushed me. To keep Deborah from seeing me cry, I managed to fight back the tears. Next, Bill started throwing my clothes out the door yelling.

"Get out..., and don't ever come back! Don't want you and don't need you!"

There was nothing more for me to do but to grant him his wishes. I picked up my scattered clothes from off the hallway floor and jumped in my van. My unfocussed mind left me in a daze while I drove as fast as possible. All of a sudden, at the twinkling of an eye, my life flew pass me. I swerved to the left, just in time, to keep from running into a long pickup truck carrying coal to the mill. My life almost ended. I can't quite explain it, but it seemed like someone or something took over the steering wheel "with the quickness."

My heart raced while pulling over to the side to get myself together. I grabbed a paper towel and wiped my sweaty face while taking deep breaths trying to calm down. Sitting there made me think about my life, which had no meaning. I wanted to change, but didn't quite have the strength to do so. I was slowly, but surely becoming numb to being in an abusive relationship. However, I gave thanks to whom thanks is due for sending an angel to my rescue.

My focus quickly went to Tina. I longed to do better as a mother and see my child grow up. I was grateful for my parent's being good role models. They stood in the gap.

They knew that Bill was still in my life, but wasn't aware of the extent of my pain and suffering. There was no need for them to know. In all likelihood, I would have been upset with them if they tried to interfere.

A lot of weight was on my shoulders. I got myself into this mess and needed to have the will power to get myself out of this ordeal.

I was glad that everyone was in bed when arriving home. Going straight to bed was of essence to me. It's amazing what a good night's sleep can do.

A few days went by before Bill called me. He begged me to come back.

I said, "You've put me through hell and now you're asking me to come back?"

"Sorry, you should know me by now. You challenged me and made me say those things. Ain't mean it, though. Hey, let's take Tina to the movies, and then go out to dinner, my treat. Sarah, I really care bout you. If I didn't, I wouldn't be beggin' you to come back."

I had mixed emotions about going back. I was "sick and tired of being sick and tired." The magnet seemed to pull me back again. It was a mistake. The cycle of abuse started over after "putting my foot in my mouth" accusing him of another woman. Bill snapped once again.

Using obscenities he said, "You ain't gettin' it. I thought you would have learned by now. I guess I have to prove what happens to girls like you!"

His demeanor turned frightening…

I tried to run towards the door, but Bill caught me. He pushed me toward the sink while I pleaded for mercy. Then he reached under the sink and grabbed a jumper cable. Why they were there is beyond my imagination. He tied me to the sink with the cables and proceeded to torture me. I started screaming, so he gagged my mouth so no one could hear me. He tied the other end of the jumper cables to the faucet and told me, I'd better not move. All of a sudden, my body fluids became uncontrollable and began to take flight.

Without saying a word about it, Bill slapped me. While igniting a feeling of power, he said, "I'm goin' to electrocute you…. I'll teach you a lesson or two…."

I was helpless and frightened out of my wits while thinking this might be the end. What he said to me next, completely blew my mind.

"Do you know who you dealing wit? Do you? The police are lookin' for me and my wife for armed robbery and violation of probation in New York. And that ain't all. You don't even wanna know the rest. Yea, I gotta rap sheet!"

Then he started laughing and laughing. The look on his face was indescribable. My chest pounded fast. I thought a heart attack was in progress. Bill tied my body so tightly that any movement was next to impossible. I was in a state of shock.

"All I got to do is wrap you up, put you in the trunk, then throw you in the river. Do not mess wit me. You hear me!"

After much ridicule, he finally calmed down and untied me. I was trembling uncontrollably. He had to shake me several times before I came out of the state of shock. Everything came back to my remembrance, including him having a wife.

Bill threatened me. He told me he'd kill me if I ever left him for another man. He said he would kill my family if word got out to anyone what he just told me. I took him at his word and didn't tell a sole.

Suddenly, there was a knock on the door. Before he opened it, he threatened me again and told me I'd better act as if everything was ok. He didn't want anyone to know what had just happened. A couple of his acquaintances came by to pick him up. They came in, covered their noses, made a face, and quickly left out.

After they left, cleaning myself up was the first thing that I did. I was still shaking like a leaf while taking a shower and wondering what to do next. I was scared to stay with him and scared to leave. The thought crossed my mind about going to the police but fear set in. All kind of questions popped up in my mind, but I didn't have the answers. I felt so all alone and had no one to help me to figure this all out. My guardian angel seemed to have deserted me.

I found out later that Bill had been married for seven years and separated for four. His wife was a prostitute living in New York and strung out on drugs. The reason they never filed for a divorce was that they both had criminal records and were using aliases.

Bill used two other additional names. His real name was Harry Wilson. When I met him, he told me his name was Bill Taylor. Claude Fields was another alias of his. He used the name Bill Taylor to collect welfare checks and used the name Claude Fields whenever he got in trouble with the police. I don't know how he got away with it. He had false identifications made up, and really covered his tracks. I wondered whether his other associates knew about his aliases. If they did, no one seemed to care, not even Tracy.

CHAPTER ELEVEN

BILL HAD ANOTHER ACQUAINTANCE, TRACY WILLIS, who gave me many headaches. She came to his room frequently disregarding the fact of me living there. If we were in the bar together, she would show off to make sure I heard whatever she said about me. Making a scene in public was not my character, so I tried to ignore her until it was next to impossible.

I followed her to the restroom in the bar, one evening. "If you got anything to say about me, say it to my face!" I snarled. I felt awkward looking down on her face because she was so much shorter.

The stocky midget swore at me, and the scuffle was on. We started fighting like cats and dogs until the bartender came in and broke it up. The battle wasn't over yet, so we went outside and started fighting again. This time Bill broke it up and started yelling at us. Then he made both of us get into the van and took us to his apartment. I assumed that he was going to make us apologize to each other.

Instead, Bill said, "Since y'all wanna fight, how bout finishin' this here, right now!"

Against our wishes, Bill pushed us into fighting again. Because of my height, I had complete advantage and beat the crap out of her. However, she scratched my face up and pulled a chunk of my hair out. My face began to sting. We were both exhausted as she got up and left.

Immediately, Bill jumped on me and busted my lip. He said I deserved it. While putting pressure on my bleeding mouth with a paper towel, he escorted me back to the bar. My lip swelled up. After seeing the disfigurement of my mouth, everybody thought Tracy "jacked" me up. I felt so humiliated and begged Bill to take me home.

Bill took me back to the apartment and gave me a towel for my face. I dampened the towel with cool water and patted my burning skin. He gave me an ice pack to put on my swollen lip. We never said a word to each other the rest of the night.

Bill could tell that I was getting frustrated and ready to leave him again, so he started sticking around the house more. He started being extra nice while thinking of a reason to keep me there.

I started getting sick. For a while, I thought it was stress related. There was no reason for me to complain to Bill. He was not the sympathetic type. The same symptoms went on for weeks, usually in the morning. I was tired all the time and started missing a lot of work.

After finally making it to the doctor, he gave me a pregnancy test. The results were positive. I didn't know whether to be happy or sad and was too sick to feel any kind of emotion. Waiting to tell Bill, when he was in a good mood, seemed to take forever. Finally, the opportunity presented itself.

We were watching a movie late one night when I blurted, "Bill, you know I've been sick a lot lately? Well, when I went to the doctor, they decided to give me a pregnancy test. It's positive. I'm six weeks pregnant." I showed him the paper from the doctor's office to prove it.

"All right! My girl!" Bill said as he gave me a "high five". He was happy, so happy. He could hardly wait to spread the news. "I want a girl, and I will be the best dad in the world. Just wait and see cause it's you and me now, 'babe.' Things goin' change for the better."

He bought a box of cigars and started giving them out. Unfortunately, his happy-go-lucky attitude didn't last too long. In a few days, he was back to his old behavior.

I had to work daylight the next morning. While asleep, Bill used his keys to open the door. Then he turned the light on which blurred my vision. At times, he could be so inconsiderate. I glanced at the clock and noticed it was 2:30 a.m.

I heard a female's voice, which startled me. I looked up and saw Shirley Duncan. I tried my best not to get upset. Due to my pregnancy, Bill had made a promise not to mistreat or disrespect me anymore. He told me not to provoke him if I wanted a peaceful relationship.

I had never encountered any problems with Shirley before. She always respected me. She knew Bill was my man.

"Hi, Shirley."

"Hi, Sarah," she said, while looking at Bill and waiting for him to say something.

"Sarah, Shirley is goin' stay here tonight? She missed her last bus. The next one ain't coming till 8 a.m. She can sleep on the couch."

My response wouldn't have mattered. Bill would have done whatever he wanted to do anyway. Heavy-eyed, but still trying to be polite, I asked them if they were hungry. They both said they were starving. I got up and fixed a quick breakfast, which consisted of a bacon, egg, and cheese omelet, hash brown potatoes, toast, and orange juice.

After finishing up, I got back into the bed to get a few more hours of sleep. I did not feel like doing any dishes that time of the morning. They stayed up and played cards. At least, they were quiet.

When the alarm went off, Bill was snoring. Shirley was on the couch "so-called" asleep. I ate some cereal, fixed myself a lunch, and got ready for work.

A nagging feeling surfaced in my mind that something wasn't right, so I purposely left my work clothes. In exactly 10 minutes, I was back tiptoeing in the hall of the apartment building while quietly unlocking the door. That quick, Bill and Shirley were in bed together. They were stunned to look up and see me standing there.

I was outraged and cussed Bill out. "You no-good.... I thought you changed. I thought I could trust you. The only reason I came back was because I forgot my work clothes!"

I looked at Shirley with disgust and said, "You're a tramp. I tried to be kind to you and look at the thanks I get. Get the hell out of here!"

Bill jumped up, threw on his shorts, and pushed me out of the room. He threw my work clothes in the hall while he cussed me out and called me every name in the book.

I never wanted his women friends to see or hear me crying so I picked my things up and left.

While in a hurry to work, the emotional pain became unbearable. It showed on my job. My performance was not up to par that day. I told my boss I was sick. He excused me for the rest of the day. I headed straight to my parents' house.

That should have been the icing on the cake to end the relationship for good. I began to realize that where there is no trust, there's no foundation. Yet, my heart wanted to forgive him once again and try to work things out. I said a little prayer while driving home:

> *God, I am doing everything possible to please this man. I have given him the benefit of the doubt so many times. As you see, I'm trying to trust him even when I shouldn't. Now that I'm I'm carrying his child, a part of me just can't seem to let go. For some reason, I never could let go. God, I truly love this man. Please forgive him. Now, I know, that you know, that I haven't done everything right myself, and I'm truly sorry, but right now, I need a big favor from you. Can you please change him a little so that we can be one big happy family? Please God. Amen!*

My parents always said that God hears prayers. I wanted to see for myself. The situation should be changing any day. I waited and waited for the results. Instead of things getting better, they got worse.

I began to question the Lord:

Where are you Lord? Did you not hear me? Did you forget about me? I didn't get an answer nor did I feel anything.

Bill asked me if he could take the van to New York. When he approached me, his cousins were with him.

I calmly said, "No, I don't want my van being used as a "drug lug." I knew Bill wanted to use it for illegal activity.

Bill called me a name and said, "You tellin' your man, no? Well, I'm gonna take it anyway!" He glared at me for a hot second. Next, he snatched my glasses off my face and punched me in the eye. My vision became fuzzy. I put my hand over my eyes.

"I am calling the police on you!"

That statement was a mistake. He became extremely hostile. After throwing me on the ground and spitting in my face, he said, "Don't no woman ever tell me they callin' the police on me and get away wit it!"

I tried to get up to run but wasn't quick enough. Bill snatched me and took the metal chain that was on the inside door of the van and wrapped it around my neck. He tied the other end to the back door. He threw me in the back of the van, and we were off to New York along with his friends to buy drugs to bring back and sell.

When we arrived at the gasoline station, the chain was still around my neck. I vomited all in the back of the van. Bill pulled over to the side of the road, cussed me out some more, and made me clean it up. There were rags and disinfectant stored in a bucket.

Not one of his "homies" showed any type of compassion or attempt to help me. One of them offered me a soda. I flat out refused. It was an insult. They should not have allowed him to throw me in that van and take me on their deceitful, illegal drug pickup. They knew I was pregnant but showed no concern about Bill possibly jeopardizing my baby's life. Nor did they seem to care about the possibility of the police stopping us and finding drugs. I would have been an accessory to a crime since the van was in my name. If I wasn't so afraid of the consequences, I would have thrown that can of soda at each one of their fatheads.

My eye was bruised and swollen. When we arrived at the rest stop, Bill took the chain off so I could use the restroom. This was the only time he untied me while positioning himself outside the door. This made it impossible for me to make phone calls, talk to anyone, or run.

When we finally arrived back home, I nursed my eye and waited until it looked satisfactory. Going to the doctor was the next step. Fortunately, the baby was fine. I was afraid to tell anyone what happened.

Bill continued to go back and forth to New York with the van to buy drugs and transport them back to sell. I did not say a word.

At six months into my pregnancy, I took a maternity leave from my job. The benefits received later weren't adequate. I was accustomed to having more money and Bill knew it. Therefore, he tried to convince me to start selling drugs.

"Hey 'babe,'" Bill said, as we were sitting on the couch watching television. He held my hand as he continued to talk. "You always tellin' me how much you love me, and I know you do. Well, your man needs your help now."

"What's wrong now? You look so serious."

Bill got up and began to pace the floor. "Honey, I'm in a big bind and don't know what else to do. I owe Jerry and other people some dough. I lost my drugs, but they ain't tryin' to hear that. I can't re-up and get my next package till I pay up."

I interrupted and said, "I would love to help you pay them back, but you know my income is limited. I'm on sick leave, remember?"

Bill replied politely, "Oh, no, honey, I ain't asking you to pay my debt. I'm a man and I can definitely straighten this thing out." Then he looked at me with those dark-brown eyes.

"Sarah, how about you buyin' a package and sellin' it? You don't use drugs, so I know you could make some fast cash."

I stood up and looked at him with disbelief. "Are you crazy? I don't know the first thing about buying and selling drugs and you want me to do something like that?"

Bill stood up, put his hand on my shoulder, and looked me dead in the eyes. "Please do it for me, 'babe,' just till I get on my feet. I promise, it ain't goin' take long, and you ain't never got to do this again."

I stood my grounds. "I am not jeopardizing myself and end up going to jail. I love you, but can't do it. I have a daughter as well as a child on the way to think about."

I started to tell him to get one of his other women to do it but decided to keep my mouth shut.

Bill sat back down with a disappointed look on his face. He was unusually quiet the next few days. Witnessing him not going out the house became the surprising part of the whole ordeal. If someone came to the door for him, he told me to say he was not here. I wasn't used to him being this way. He seemed to be hiding from someone.

During the time of his hibernation, he ate very little and seemed to be constantly sick. I placed a bucket by his bed. He vomited quite often. As fast as I cleaned the bucket out, he threw up again. I stayed in and witnessed the fact he hadn't done any drugs. When he had the shakes, it worried me, so I asked him if he needed to go to the hospital.

He ferociously replied, "No!" He said that he would be all right after awhile, so I just placed a warm blanket over him as well as a cold rag on his forehead.

Bill was very edgy. I catered to him and was determined not to leave his side. He didn't talk much, so comforting him as much as possible was all I knew to do. Finally, after several days of Bill feeling under the weather, he was able to keep some food down in his system. I made him some homemade chicken noodle soup. The aroma went all down the hall. Bill sat up for the first time after being ill all week.

"Thank you for being by my side. I love you, girl."

"I love you too, Bill." I sat there in "awe" and could not remember the last time he said those words to me.

I quietly thanked God for answering my prayer.

His attitude towards me seemed to get a little better after this crisis. He treated me with a little more respect. For the first time, in a while, I felt appreciated. After seven days of being in the house with Bill and thinking things over, I made a decision to sit down and have a talk with him.

"I've been thinking about what we talked about last week, and will do what you asked of me. I will try to make us some quick money just this one time so that you can get back on your feet. I don't know what I'm doing so you have to help me out." I was worried that the people he owed would come after him.

Bill looked at me and just smiled. He suddenly seemed to get a boost of energy. His face lit up. He was happy.

Over the course of time, Bill taught me the ropes of selling drugs. I learned how to weigh and bag up as well as the charging price. He also informed me of the games people play to try to "get over." What I didn't know was that one day I would become my own best customer. I did not realize the consequences of dealing drugs.

I started out selling marijuana after weighing and bagging it up. Selling nickel and dime bags wasn't turning the money over fast enough for Bill.

After a while, we started selling larger packages. My customers could not come to the house. They had to catch up with me in the streets. I thought things were moving smoothly, but Bill didn't seem to think so. He said I was making "chump change."

"Now Sarah, you been sellin' weed for bout a month now and we ain't got ahead."

I boldly replied, "That's because you keep taking the profit."

"Oh no, don't blame me. We ain't makin' no money cause you keep givin' it away. I know for a fact you been givin' it to your sister. Somebody told me. Look, let's finish sellin' what we got and get some cocaine to sell. We can make triple the profit, and it's a quicker turnaround."

"That's even worse! People will rob you for that." I stated.

Bill put his arms around me. "Didn't you say you love me and will do anything for me?"

I nodded.

"Well, I got your back. Trust me on this one. Since you pregnant, you can't test it. When we buy it, I will test it to make sho it ain't junk. I'll even bag it up for you. When I make a sale, I'll bring you the cash. Okay? By this time next month, we can quit and be well on our feet."

I had second thoughts on doing this, but held my peace. Something he said didn't sound right but I couldn't figure it out. It went right over my head.

At first, the drug money seemed good. I was able to put some to the side. Then, the drugs started mysteriously disappearing. I would hide it in my drawer underneath different clothes. When going back for it, it was completely gone, or a good bit of it was missing. On top of that, Bill constantly asked me for money. If I didn't give it to him, he became very hostile. The circumstances began to be too stressful, so I quit. This was not for me. I needed to focus more on settling before the birth of our baby.

CHAPTER TWELVE

SEVEN MONTHS INTO MY PREGNANCY gave me enough time to save a little money. My focus centered on finding a house. I bought a weekly newspaper and began searching for rental property.

After carefully searching for a few weeks, we found one to our satisfaction. The seven room two-story house had aluminum siding. On the first floor, there was a nice-sized living room, sitting room, dining room, kitchen, and powder room. On the second floor, there were three large bedrooms and a master bathroom. The house looked much nicer on the inside than the outside. The large front porch and small back yard meant less grass cutting.

The property owner told me the remodeled house on 1304 Maple Drive was approximately one hundred years old. This house consisted of old-fashioned heaters and slightly slanted floors in two rooms on the first level of the house. Nonetheless, for a starter, there was no reason to complain. The rent was $180.00 a month plus utilities. Everything seemed to be falling in place. We had a van, a house, and I was pregnant with his child.

Before Bill moved in, he said, "I'm kind of wonderin' if I should move in wit you or not. You might get mad at me and have me put out."

"Bill, that's the last thing you have to worry about. I would never do that. You allowed me to live with you even though we had our problems, so I think I can do the same for you. We have a child on the way that we need to think about as well as Tina, and last, but not least, I really do love you."

Deep in my heart, I now believed we had a better chance than ever to work at making our relationship the best it could be.

For a while, Bill shared my enthusiasm. He treated me with the love I have been longing for. He did everything I asked him to do. It was as if he couldn't do enough for me. On occasion, he washed and folded up the laundry and even ran my bath water.

Bill began spending a lot of quality time with me. The other women didn't seem to be in the picture any more. We laughed and had so much fun. He did a good job when he painted the rooms, too.

The day after Bill first painted; Lorraine and I were bringing some items into the new house. We had to be careful because of our pregnancies. We weren't aware that Bill was hiding upstairs. It was around 9 p.m., and dark outside. I turned on the light in the living room, dining room, and kitchen. All of a sudden, there was a noise of something tumbling down the steps coming from the second floor.

Lorraine and I looked at each other. Her eyes widened. She gasped, held her breath, and grabbed my arm. She whispered something, jokingly, about the place being haunted.

"All I know is nothing else better not come tumbling down those stairs," said Lorraine.

All of a sudden, something did. We ran out of the house, pregnant bellies and all screaming to the top of our lungs. Just then, Bill came out of the house laughing uncontrollably. We laughed with him after realizing the prank he played.

On the following day, after thoroughly cleaning the house, Bill and I moved in our clothes. We purchased used furniture from the second- hand store that was within my budget. My life, my home, and my soon-to-be born baby gave me such a good feeling of a fresh-new start. New furniture could wait.

My next agenda was to work on Tina's bedroom, so she could move in and have her own space. Even though she liked the show, "The Animals Neighborhood," she really loved anything that had to do with a princess. Therefore, I brought her princess curtains, sheets, and blankets. It took a while for me to find a lamp with a matching clock. Next, I bought her new clothes and toys for her to enjoy in her new home. She was now six years old.

My mom, reluctantly, gave Tina up. Nonetheless, she was a woman of her word. She promised she would give Tina back to me when I get my own place.

I stopped at the house before mom left to go to choir rehearsal. Dad was at work. I came at that particular time to avoid a long drawn-out conversation and showed mom the rent receipt.

"I finally got things together mom. I found a house on Maple Drive right down the street from Mark's house. It's a nice house. And I fixed up Tina's room. I would like to come and get her this weekend if that's alright with you."

Mom seemed happy about my getting my own place but wanted to make sure that I knew what I was doing. She seemed a little saddened about letting Tina go.

Mom questioned me. "How much is the rent?" Can you afford it?"

"Yes, my rent is only one hundred and eighty dollars a month. When I get my income tax, I'm going to pay six months in advance."

Mom said. "Well, I hope you do because I don't have any money to be paying no back rent." Then she looked at me and asked, "Are you still messing with that boy? I heard some things that were not good."

I defended him. "We used to have a lot of problems, but he's has been treating me okay lately. He's changed a lot."

Firmly, mom said, "Okay, I'm taking you for your word, but I better not hear that he's down there mistreating you or Tina. If I find out anything differently, if I have to, I will take you to court to get Tina back."

That remark was not to my liking but I knew it would be best for me to let it go. I was hoping she didn't ask me any more questions. Unfortunately, that was not the case.

Mom said, "Oh, by the way, don't you have something to tell me?"

I gave her a puzzled look. Wearing large size clothes didn't help the least bit. Lying about this wouldn't have done me any good either because my belly was showing "big as day." More than likely, Lorraine must have told her.

"Yes, I'm pregnant." Admitting it made me feel so ashamed. She had instilled good morals in me, and I let her down once again.

Mom confessed, "I knew it all the time. You didn't fool me not one bit. You need Jesus!"

I left while my disappointed mom was getting Tina's things together. On Friday, I came back to pick her up and was so excited to finally have my daughter back.

Bill played with Tina a lot. He was a lot of fun at times, and Tina really liked him. There was no need for her, as well as my parent's, to know the truth about Bill at this time. I kept many things to myself to keep from involving them. Whenever there were noticeable bruises on my face, staying away from them, as well as the public eye, seemed to be the best solution. Giving them information about my bad relationship would have given them a reason to give me advice that would have gone in one ear and out the other. There was no need for them to worry about me.

The last woman that I had to deal with concerning Bill was Donna Ferezza. She was a fair complexion middle-aged woman with a fake mole on her right cheek. She wore a lot of make-up that helped offset her smooth skin tone. When going out to a party or cabaret, she dressed very nice.

Donna was a self-employed beautician. Many of her patrons would come to her house. She had two children, a three-year-old girl, and a five-year-old boy. She had a great personality and was very friendly with anyone she met.

Bill spent nights with Donna on occasion. He conveyed to me they were just very good friends. Although he tried to convince me that all they did was play cards all night, it did not set well with me. I would still get upset when he stayed overnight at her house. Bill could care less about my thoughts or the emotional turmoil he was putting me through.

"Bill, you are spending too much time at Donnas'," I complained.

"How many times I gotta say this, that's my friend. I told you over and over all we do is play cards all night. Why can't you get that in your thick skull? You need to just come see for your-self because I am sick and tired of explainin' this bull crap!"

For some reason, Bill wanted Donna and me to be good friends. Whenever we were in the bar together, if he was with me, she seemed to get mad. If he was with her, I would get mad. He finally beckoned her to come and speak to me to break the ice. Donna came willingly.

"Hi, Sarah. How are you doing?"

"Fine," I said rather sharply, while looking the other way. Donna was persistent in trying to get a conversation out of me.

"Bill told me you're pregnant. He's so proud. He said he can't wait."

"Yeah, I'll be glad when this is all over too. I'm glad I don't have morning sickness anymore."

Donna said, "Have you gotten anything for the baby yet?"

"My mom's buying the crib for me. Next week, I'm going to buy a bassinet and a stroller. I already have blankets and undershirts and stuff like that. I haven't bought any clothes because I don't know if I'm having a boy or a girl."

"Well, is it okay if I buy a couple of big bags of Pampers?"

"Sure, that would be appreciated." Bill had walked away to talk to some friends, so Donna and I continued to talk about different things.

"Hey Sarah, do you ever go Bingo?"

"No. I never was interested in it."

"Well, I'm going tomorrow. Would you like to come? You'd probably be lucky since it will be your first time. Like they say, beginners luck."

I hesitated before answering. I didn't exactly want to be her hangout partner. "Well, ok, I don't have anything to do on tomorrow. Besides, it would be a change for me. I'll get my sister-in-law to baby sit Tina. What time should I pick you up?" I knew Donna didn't have a car.

"I guess around 6. I want to be there for the early jackpot."

We began going to bingo together. Surprisingly, it was a lot of fun and kept my mind occupied from focusing on Bill so much. I needed a change in my thinking process anyway.

The first time we went to bingo, I did not win any money. So much for beginner's luck Donna was talking about. However, after going for a while, luck began to come my way.

After socializing with Donna more and more, I realized she was a cool person. I had many opportunities to see how she reacted with other people. She had the "gift of gab" with anyone she met. If anyone was feeling down, including me, she knew the right words to encourage or cheer you up. Because of her genuine personality, I felt comfortable enough to confide in her about certain matters concerning Bill.

Donna also played the numbers a lot and soon it rubbed off on me. A few times, I hit for a small amount. One day, I hit the Big-Four straight and won $2,500.00. That was a lot for me, and it couldn't have happened at a better time.

Bill's plan worked. Donna and I managed to become good friends. His next plan entailed bringing her to our house. He was a very controlling person, and it seemed that everything had to go his way. Opening my mouth about certain matters, would result in Bill embarrassing me, so I tried my best to be polite. Generally, we would play cards, Parcheesi, or checkers, which was my favorite. Other times, we just watched a movie on TV or talked about different things.

Many times, Bill disrespected me around Donna. He would carry on a conversation with her acting as if I didn't exist. If I butted in, sometimes he would call me names and say he wasn't talking to me.

"What... are you sittin' there lookin' stupid for?"

Then he turned to Donna. "Can't stand her and her childish attitude."

Countless times, I just sat there. It hurt so much on the inside when he said things like that. If he didn't get his way, or I got smart with him, he often jumped on me. It didn't matter that she was there. Donna would try to pull him off me, but to no avail.

"Leave her alone Bill. You're going to hurt the baby!"

Bill shouted, "Stay out of it Donna. This ain't none of your ...business. See what I mean, every time I try bein' nice, Sarah wanna get stupid. Should be glad to know where I'm at and what I'm doin. She ain't never satisfied."

Bill turned his attention towards me. "I've had it wit you. I'm outa here." He grabbed the keys to the van, walked out, and took Donna home.

I was home, alone and miserable, and didn't see him until the next evening. He came in, changed his clothes, and left again. Never once did he ask me how I was feeling. He didn't seem to care.

While I was pregnant, Bill did just about everything to me except hit me in the stomach. Stress became a normal part of my life. When I went to the doctor, he diagnosed me as being anemic. He immediately admitted me into the hospital.

Bill came home and I wasn't there. He searched for me. My family didn't tell him that I was in the hospital. Bill didn't find out about my whereabouts until three days later.

He came into my hospital room, furious, and called me out of my name. "What…. are you doin' here?"

I got upset about the way he was talking to me, and chose not to answer him. He asked me a second time. I refused to respond. Within seconds, he punched me in my mouth.

"I know why you here! You gettin' rid of our kid, ain't you?" Before I could respond, he said, "I'll kill you if you do!"

He started choking me. I screamed. The nurses called security, and they escorted Bill out of the hospital. He could not to return for the remainder of my hospital stay. Because of the stress related incident, the doctor kept me for a couple of extra days. He suggested I get a "Protection Against Cruelty Order" against Bill as soon as possible.

The next day, Bill called me on the phone weeping. That was the first time I ever heard him cry.

"Sorry, I feel like a fool. I ain't been myself lately. I thought you been in the hospital gettin' rid of our baby. Please let me make this up to you."

I screamed on the phone and said, "I didn't tell you that I was in the hospital because I needed a rest from you!" Bill got quiet.

When it was time for me to go home, the doctor's main order was for me to get plenty of rest. I carefully explained the situation to Bill, but instead, he stressed me out even more and continued bringing his women friends to my house or staying out all night. The mental as well as physical abuse increased, and I was concerned for the baby's well-being. I had no other choice but to take the doctor's advice and start procedures for a "Protection Against Cruelty Order."

91

Petition for Protection Against Cruelty Order

And now comes the petitioner, Sarah Jones, by her Attorneys and Domestic Legal Rights Association, respectfully represents the following:

1)   The petitioner, Sarah Jones, is an adult individual residing at 1304 Maple Drive, Englewood, Colorado, 80113.

2)   The respondent, William Bill Taylor, is an adult individual residing at 1304 Maple Drive, Englewood, Colorado, 80113.

3)   The resident of petitioner and respondent is rented.

4)   Petitioner at present is unemployed.

5)   Petitioner is the natural parent of one child, Tina, age 6, and she is presently seven months pregnant.

6)   On numerous occasions beginning nearly 1 year ago, and continuing to the present, respondent has struck and threatened petitioner. On one occasion in July of 1980, the respondent put a metal chain around the neck of the petitioner, choking her.

7)   Very recently on August 26, 1980, while petitioner was in the hospital undergoing tests concerning her pregnancy, respondent struck petitioner with his full fist causing her mouth to bleed.

8)   Soon after petitioner was released from the hospital on or about September 5, 1980,

responded again struck petitioner in the face, this incident occurring at the residence.

9)   The most recent incident, which placed petitioner in fear of imminent serious bodily harm, occurred on September 10, 1980. At this time respondent threatened to kill petitioner and destroy the residence.

10)   Respondent's attacks have placed petitioner in fear of imminent bodily harm for herself   and   her   unborn   child.

Wherefore, the petitioner prays that the Court grant her prayer by granting sole possession of the premises at 1304 Maple Drive, Englewood, Colorado to her and her child, and by granting such relief as is provided for her by the Protection Against Cruelty Order.

Respectfully Submitted:

Thomas Jatah
Attorney for Petitioner

When Bill received his papers, he sent word that something bad was going to happen if I didn't drop the charges. When the court date came, I decided not to show up. Shortly after, I received a letter from the court:

Dear Miss Jones:

Due to failure to attend a hearing before Judge Weston on September 19, 1980, the order of court excluding William Bill Taylor from your residence is no longer in effect, and Mr. Tailor can enter your residence at 1304

Maple Drive without being in violation of the preliminary order.

If you have any questions, please contact me at this office.

Yours truly,
Jeff Wyler
Domestic Legal Rights Association

Lucky for Bill, things turned out in his favor, which should have made him happy. Instead, he was the total opposite.

When Bill walked into the house, he had that certain-menacing look on his face. No doubt, he was ready to put me through fierce turmoil. He began the cycle by closing the windows and locking the door, and pulling all the phone plugs out the jacks. Trouble was evident and I had to think fast.

While he was fumbling with the windows, I ran upstairs to search for his pistol. I was tired of taking the beatings. The .32 caliber handgun was underneath the mattress. The fact of me knowing absolutely nothing about guns should have scared me enough not to touch it. At the time, my thinking wasn't straight.

"Bill!" I yelled. When he looked up, my hands were trembling as I pointed the gun at him. The look on his face was beyond words in the English language. He swerved and ducked. You would have thought he was doing one of his made-up dances with a new rhythm.

Within a few seconds, he grabbed the pistol. Unfortunately, I would not let go. We were both under pressure to gain control. Sweat poured down Bill's face while he cursed "up a storm." In a matter of time, I became the weakest link.

Bill looked at me strangely and then pinned me to the wall. "I don't believe this. You tried to shoot me...! You better be glad you pregnant. If you ever in yo life try that stupid stuff again, I'm gonna make you regret the day you were born!"

From that day on, he never kept his gun where I could find it. My plans were not to shoot him. I just wanted to scare him and let him know that enough is enough.

Bill looked into the chamber and pulled out the bullets. That gun could have accidentally gone off and someone could have been in jail, hurt, or dead.

Later, that night, I thanked God for protecting me and promised never to do anything stupid like that again.

For the next couple of months, Bill refrained from putting his hands on me. I was relieved because the baby was due any day.

CHAPTER THIRTEEN

I HOPED FOR A GIRL AND BILL'S choice was a boy. Either way, it did not matter as long as our child was healthy. Prior to my first labor pain, I cleaned the house from top to bottom. By late evening, taking a nap was necessary. All of a sudden, around 9 p.m., a sharp pain hit me, and I let out one big ouch. The ache subsided and my first thought was false labor. My due date wasn't until two more weeks. By the time I dozed off again, another tremendous pain hit me in my belly. I sat straight up and reached for the phone.

Calling around looking for Bill was a little aggravating. The time for the birth of our child was getting close; therefore, he should have been reachable. Bill had assured me repeatedly that he would be there to see our baby arrive into this world.

Another excruciating pain came. While watching the clock, I took notice that the contractions were fifteen minutes apart. There were messages left with different people who might see Bill to tell him to hurry home. The time had come for me to go to the hospital.

He called me on the phone an hour later. "Hey, got your message."

My pains were starting to get sharper and closer. I took a deep breath. "Bill, please come home! I'm having labor pains, and they are about six or seven minutes apart! I need you to take me to the hospital!"

Calmly, he said, "You sure it ain't false labor?"

Frantically, I screamed, "Yes, I'm sure! Please hurry! I need to go to the hospital now!"

Bill was home within 10 minutes. I was relieved he wasn't high.

Instead of being sympathetic towards me, he broke out and said, "You mind if Donna come to the hospital wit us?"

I looked at him in a state of disbelief without uttering a single word. This precious moment should have been something just for Bill and me to share.

He held my arm as I wobbled to the van. All of a sudden, my water broke. Bill ran in the house, grabbed some towels, and laid them on the seat.

Regardless of the sensitivity of my feelings and the horrific pain, Bill stopped and picked up Donna anyway. Afterwards, he started driving like a maniac. I didn't speak to Donna when she got into the car. Unfortunately, it didn't stop her from babbling. She seemed to be at her peak.

After we got to the hospital, the severe labor pains continued approximately four more hours. Bill received permission to be in the delivery room. Donna stayed in the waiting room but would come in and check on me from time to time. In spite of everything I had been through with Bill, his being by my side gave me confidence of getting through the birth of our child.

The nurse gave Bill a scrub outfit to put on. He pretended to be a professional doctor. I laughed for a quick second at his outrageous appearance. After that, my smile changed back to a frown. The sharp pains began to be more than I could bear. Every time they hit me, I hollered and squeezed Bill's hand tightly. The truth of the matter is--I really wanted to break every bone in his hand for putting me through this.

When those undesirable moments came, I began yelling for help and begged for pain medication. For some reason, unbeknownst, the doctor refused to give me anything. I vomited all over the place. After that subsided, I wanted to sucker punch the doctor.

Bill calmly said, "Breathe in, breathe out." He repeated those words numerous times.

When the baby's head came out, the doctor told me to push.

Bill said, "Come on Sarah, push!" He encouraged me the rest of the way.

It seemed like eternity, but the baby was finally out. The doctor showed Bill how to cut the cord. We birthed a beautiful baby girl. She was seven pounds, fourteen ounces, and twenty-two inches long. She had a head full of jet-black silky hair.

Bill named her Alisha Wilson. He was determined to give her his real last name. He seemed so overjoyed and so was I--now that it was over. After the nurses cleaned her up, Bill held her. While he gently embraced our baby, Bill turned facing the wall. He took out a handkerchief, and wiped his eyes. After he left the hospital, he went home and celebrated. I heard he got drunk.

The hospital released me three days later. Bill picked me up and upon my arrival at home; the house was surprisingly super clean. There were roses waiting for me with a card that said, "To My Special Lady, I'm Yours Forever." He wrote a note on the card that said, "Thank you for givin' me my own little baby princess."

I felt a moment of happiness and said, "You're welcome."

Bill helped us settle in. I showed him how to make baby formula. He was very handy, except when she had a messy diaper. Bill didn't want anything to do with that. I'm grateful that he made sure everything was reachable to keep me from moving around a lot.

Alisha was no doubt daddy's little girl, and he gave her lots of hugs and kisses.

Alisha grew rather fast and began to look more and more like her father. She was a very pleasant baby unless she was hungry. As fast as I put a spoonful of baby food in her mouth, she screamed for more and gulped it down like there was no tomorrow.

For the first several months, Alisha faithfully woke up every two hours. Bill refused to get up with her. If I took too long getting out of the bed to see about the baby, Bill would yell at me. There were many nights of being extremely exhausted. Bill could care less. Occasionally, I asked him to get up, change her, and give her a bottle. I needed to get a little more rest. To him, this small request was out of the question.

Tina would often wake up in the middle of the night from hearing the baby cry or from Bill yelling at me. Cutting her television on helped her soon drift back to sleep.

Tina adored Alisha and was not jealous of her at all. "Mommy, can I hold my baby sister?"

"Of course you can, but since she's so little, you have to sit still." I showed Tina how to make sure her arm was around the back of Alisha's neck.

"I think she's hungry. Why don't you give her a bottle?" Tina was so happy to be helpful.

She smiled and said, "Okay, Mommy." A few minutes later, Tina said, "Mommy, mommy, the baby is wet. Can I change her?"

"Not right now, wait until she's a little older." I changed the baby and let Tina hold her for a little while longer. Alisha was soon sound asleep.

Bill spent a lot of time in the streets, but at home, his playful attitude with the kids seemed to have an advantage over his shortcomings. However, at times when he was in one of his foul moods, he made statements that were "uncalled for."

"I ain't sure this baby is mine anyway. You been messin' around on me and been actin' like you were goin' to your mom's. I ain't dumb."

I was completely dumbfounded. How could he say such a thing? Bill kept track of me and usually knew my whereabouts even when we were so-called broke up. There was no way he could deny Alisha, even if he wanted to. She looked just like him. I shook my head and continued my work or activity instead of feeding into his false accusations.

When Alicia turned six months old, we were selling drugs again. I overlooked the fact that it was illegal and assumed there wouldn't be any major problems. My intentions to sell cocaine would be short termed as far as I was concerned.

Before we packaged or sold anything, I always took the children to Latisha, my brother's wife. They lived two blocks down the street. I never wanted to expose my children to an atmosphere involving criminal activity.

Therefore, here we are, selling, and if there was such a thing as a drug jackpot, we seemed to have hit it. "We were rolling." Yet, as it goes with any rush, the crash was imminent. Instead of reaping great sums of money, I found myself supplying Bill's habit more than ever. The more drugs we invested in, the greater his habit.

At times, Bill became a little envious when he realized I kept a stash of money unlike him. "Sarah, you think you better than me, huh?"

"What in the world are you talking about? Why would you say that?"

Bill glared at me and said, "Just cause you made a little doe, you think you all that. Well, you're not."

"I don't think anything. I just don't want drugs in my body. Enjoying life is not being high. I would like to enjoy my two children without being on 'cloud nine.' And furthermore, I'm afraid I'll turn out just like you!"

With any warning, Bill slapped me. "That's exactly why I ain't here half the time. Your mouth is too smart. Furthermore, you ain't nothin' but a square anyway. I ain't feelin' you no more. I need a woman in my corner that's daring, and not afraid to explore, one with a little spunk in her life. When I'm here, all you wanna do is watch TV and read. I'm sick of watchin' TV just to please you and I'm sick of your boring lifestyle!"

The little bit of boldness left in me seemed to surface. I raised my voice and poured my heart out. "Well, what do you want me to do? I'm trying to be a good woman. I keep the house clean. I cook. I've even given you my last. I've went without just so you could have. I don't understand you. It's rarely what I do, but always what I don't do. You are never satisfied when it comes down to me. You are all about yourself, and I am so tired of this. What else do you want from me?"

Bill responded aggressively. "I want you to be a woman and get high wit your man. It ain't goin' kill you to do this one time."

We went back and forth disagreeing about what the other one was saying. There seemed to be no conclusion so Bill pulled a plastic baggie out of his pocket. He went into the bathroom. When he came out, I didn't utter a word. Not knowing what else to do, I decided to grab a magazine and pretend to read it. I was a little nervous.

He snatched the magazine out of my hand and yelled, "Look at me when I'm talkin' to you, and don't you dare start that silly cryin'. I ain't done a thang to you. I'm gonna tell you just like it is!" Bill snatched me up by both arms and demanded my full attention.

Bill calmed his voice down a notch and said, "Look, Girl, either you wit me or you're not. Which one is it?"

"I'm with you, Bill." I started coughing but he didn't care.

"Then act like it, "Tackhead"!" Right after that, he made a phone call. I felt manipulated. One of his friends came over with a pipe. He put cocaine in the pipe and lit it. Bill told me how good it makes you feel, and if I didn't like it, I didn't have to do it anymore.

I was extremely nervous now not knowing what to expect. I've heard of too many people getting habits. Bill would not let up and was all in my ear. He blew smoke in my face.

His exact words were, "Take a chance, "babe." That's what it's all bout. You sellin' this stuff so you need to know for yourself what you got. You need to know if you got a good product or a bad one. Come on, Sarah. Just try it this one time. You got my word. I'll never ask again."

As he put the pipe up to my mouth, I grudgingly inhaled it and started choking.

Bill got angry and said, "You wasting...!" Then he put the pipe to my mouth again. I was vulnerable and took another hit. This time was different. Bill glared at me waiting to see my reaction. I was high and had a rush. There didn't seem to be a care in the world.

With much control over me now, Bill said, "Can I have some of your cocaine?"

I nodded. He went into my pockets and took my money and drugs. I never budged. Bill took advantage of my helpless condition. That really hurt my feelings. He didn't have to behave in such a manner.

By the time the high wore off, Bill was long gone. I felt abandoned, betrayed, and so ashamed of myself for allowing him to intimidate me into getting with his program. I chose not to pick up the children and sat on my bed feeling remorseful.

When Bill came home, we both pretended as if it never happened. Deep inside, I felt it was my fault that he took my money and drugs. Now, I am broke.

The thought crossed my mind about going to my parents and asking to borrow some money. Making ends meet until my next check would be impossible. Bills had to be paid. After what I considered careful thinking, I decided it would be best to ask the dope man to front me a package to get back on my feet. Then, I would quit.

Playing right into Bill's hands was what he expected. He continued to pressure me for drugs.

"But Bill, how do you expect me to make money if I have to give it out to you and your friends?"

"You worry too much. We'll get you more customers and make it up next time."

He had an excuse for everything. Because of his habit, I had to continue hiding everything. However, that didn't stop Bill from searching. If he didn't find what he wanted, he would check me from head to toe or snatch my purse. This repeated action caused me to take a loss most of the time, which enticed me to keep selling drugs longer than planned. I needed to get my money back and get on my feet.

As I continued along this destructive path, nothing seemed to go right. The more drugs sold, the more we used. We were freebasing as well as sniffing cocaine.

After being used to the effectiveness of the high, it wasn't so enjoyable anymore. There were times of being jittery and other times of being enormously paranoid. You couldn't tell me that the police weren't outside my door waiting to arrest me. On many occasions, I hid behind the bedroom door only to eventually realize that nobody was out there. One would think these insane issues would have made me quit using.

Unfortunately, it was not easy. I became an addict and my own best customer. Once the phase started, there was no turning back. I wanted more and more. It was a horrible nightmare. After the drugs and money were gone, I wouldn't get high anymore for a week or two until check day came. Then the senseless cycle would start all over again--starting with getting a babysitter.

On numerous occasions, I said to Bill, "This is the last time I'm selling drugs. We're using more than we're selling. After the first hit, I'm not getting any higher, so it's a total waste."

Bill always had an answer for everything. "I got a perfect solution, 'babe'. Now, don't get mad. Just hear me out. Used to feel the same way. No matter how much I used, ain't get no higher. Had to do somethin' different, so I shot up. If you like how you feel when you freebase, you'll love how it feels to shoot up. Instant high, lasts longer, and you only need a little bit." As he explained this, his speech was getting louder and faster. I saw his pupils dilate.

"Oh, no! I am afraid of needles!"

"Okay, your choice." Then he surprisingly walked away without saying anything else about it.

In the meantime, there was a battle going on in my mind and it wouldn't go away. I kept pondering about what Bill said. *If you like how you feel when you freebase, you'll love how it feels to shoot up. Instant high lasts longer, and you only need a little bit.* I tried hard to get those thoughts out of my head, but to no avail.

The continued habit of freebasing off and on resulted in me going deeper and deeper in debt. Getting ahead was impossible. There was nothing worse than smoking up hundreds of dollars of cocaine in one night without making money or getting any higher. The uncontrollable desire caused me to give in to Bill's manipulations.

"Bill," I mumbled. "Can we talk a minute?"

I wanted to get high, but couldn't afford to mess up the money. The package was getting low.

"Yea, 'babe,' what up?"

"I thought about what you said. I changed my mind. I'm willing to try this needle thing."

Bill looked pleased and said, "Thought you'd see it my way."

We went upstairs, and he pulled the black case out of his pocket, opened it, and pulled a needle out. Next, Bill put a belt around my right arm and pulled it tight. He told me to make a fist. I started shaking, and he started screaming at me.

"Be still!" The more he screamed, the more nervous I got.

"Bill, I changed my mind!" I pulled my own arm back, and that made him angrier. Sweat starting pouring off him.

"Do as I say. Shut up and be still." Bill yelled with a diabolical look on his face. 'This is what you wanted, and this is what you gonna get."

Bill grabbed my arm again, threatened me, and told me not to move. This time, he tied the belt tighter around my arm. I could not bear to look while clenching my fist and closing my eyes. My heart pounded. He stuck me several times, which made me panic and holler while he kept searching for a better vein. After finding one, he stuck the needle in.

Immediately, my ears felt like they were ringing. It was a different kind of high then freebasing and sniffing. We didn't need a lot. It was all right.

As time went on, this new phase of getting high happened more and more. The situation between us seemed to reverse. I found myself asking him if he wanted to get high. Although I was never stable enough to do it myself, mainlining was now my preference. Bill gladly did it because he could cheat me, and I was too stupid to know the difference. This went on for months and months. Drugs were getting the best of me.

I didn't like myself anymore. The bills were getting behind, and my motherly role was not as it should be. My children were going to the babysitter more often than not. My clothes sagged because of the weight loss. My face seemed to have sunk in. I looked a mess.

We went broke and didn't have any more drugs, which made Bill highly agitated. Stupidity seemed to have taken a hold of me.

Out of nowhere, Bill said, "Hey, let's take the kids to the babysitter and have some quiet time. Got a surprise for you."

I thought he had a package and wanted to get me high. I felt anxious. "Okay!"

Quickly, I put the baby in a stroller, along with formula and Pampers. Tina received a snack bag and picked a couple of her favorite toys to take with her.

Bill pushed the stroller as we walked to my brother's house. We thanked them for agreeing to babysit on such short notice. I told them if we weren't back by a certain time, they would see us first thing in the morning.

As we walked back home, Bill was unusually quiet, so I decided to break the ice. "So what's the surprise you have planned for me?" I wasn't used to getting any surprises from him. He didn't answer me.

As we got closer to the house, my thought process changed. I started to get worried and contemplated whether to go into the house. He was too close for me to take off running. I hope that my anxiety attack was just my imagination playing tricks on me.

When we went into the house, he immediately locked the door, and pulled the phone cord out the wall. I screeched and started backing up. "What's wrong? Did I do something?"

Bill quickly grabbed me and started using obscenities to emphasize his point. "I ran into your cous, Cecil, and we fought cause of you. Somebody told him I'm the reason for yo drug habit, and I'm always jumpin' on you. Who you tell that to?"

"I didn't tell anyone that, I swear I didn't!"

Bill started twisting my arm. I screamed. "Stop, you're hurting me. Let me go!"

"Shut up..., I see you ain't learned nothin' yet. Since your cous' thinks I'm beatin' you up, might as well make it true."

Bill proceeded to beat me. Screaming for help had no purpose. The closed windows kept anyone from hearing me. I pleaded and begged for mercy.

"Please stop! I'm sorry, I'm sorry!"

Bill didn't stop until he was good and tired. He was sweating, huffing, and puffing.

My body ached with pain while managing to get up from the floor. My head was pounding. Blood flowed freely from my left nostril. As I sat down and tilted my head backwards to stop the bleeding, a Kleenex box was within reach. Sitting still for fifteen minutes relieved the pressure.

Running was not an option because of my sore body. Slowly, I stood up and wobbled into the kitchen. The bottle of Tylenol was on top of the refrigerator. I felt a little dizzy, sat down, and took two pills. Bill followed me from room to room.

"I'm sorry, I'm sorry, Sarah, but you pushed me." He attempted to embrace me. I showed no response as my body stiffened up. Bill sat on the chair close to the front door to block me from running out of the house. He knew I would break camp if it were the least bit possible.

Bill wanted to go upstairs to bed, and made me go with him. I obeyed. He held me while running off at the mouth about nothing. In the middle of one of his sentences, he started snoring. While lying there, unable to sleep, my mind suddenly went back to the poem I had written.

RESCUE ME

One day as I was sitting,
Beneath the apple tree,
I looked up to the heavens,
Lonely as could be.
Asking God a question,
What is wrong with me?
Tired of making bad choices,
Come and rescue me.
I thought I heard Him say,
If you listen to the wind,
And look up at the stars,
Something deep within,
Will catch you if you fall.

Enough was enough. I shall call the police as soon as possible. Who does he think he is?

CHAPTER FOURTEEN

I WAITED A WHILE TO MAKE SURE OF THE RIGHT TIMING. Creeping down the steps without making a noise was not easy. Quickly, I called the police and then put on Bill's sunglasses. Within minutes, they banged on the door. Bill jumped up quickly and ran down the steps. He looked at me with unbelief.

The police said, "We got a call that there was a domestic problem going on here. What seems to be the problem?"

"I just want my boyfriend to leave."

The police said, "Did he hit you?"

I took one look at stern looking Bill. I replied, "No, I just want him to leave." I was afraid to tell the truth and later down the road suffer the consequences. Another reason was to keep him from going to jail. If fingerprinted, they would find out that he had a record. Once he got out of jail, he would have most likely come after me.

Before they escorted him out of the house, upon my request, they made him return my house and car keys. Bill grumbled, but complied. Eventually he would be back. I didn't trust him, so I had all the locks changed in the house.

After this incident, our relationship showed signs of tremendously going downhill. The little peace left seemed to have vanished.

However, I still held on to a little bit of faith that change was not impossible. Our biggest problem was the use of drugs and it needed to stop. If Bill would just quit, he would be a completely different person. He would be loveable, kind, and respectful toward me. Somewhere, deep inside this man, was a good-natured person, but the drugs had stolen his character.

I didn't inform Bill when the time came to return to work from my maternity leave. We were still on the "outs" but somehow, he found out. As I got into the van to go to work, he jumped out of hiding behind the seat in the back. Then he grabbed me by my neck and pulled me to the house. He must have had an extra set of car keys. Bill snatched my house keys, unlocked the front door, and pulled me in. If the neighbors saw anything, they remained oblivious. No one wanted to get involved.

I slumped over and guarded my face. To my disbelief, he didn't hit me this time. Getting back into the house and resuming the relationship was his plans. Bill allowed me to go to work after he was confident the police wasn't coming. Since I was late, the supervisor wrote me up for not calling in.

Sometimes, if we were on bad terms, Bill would hide behind my house waiting for me to come outside. Then he would jump out and attack me. Fear of staying with him had become almost as bad as the fear of breaking up with him. He always seemed to surface out of nowhere. I would be walking around the house "on pins and needles", especially when "kicking him to the curb."

On numerous occasions, I forgave him and took him back. The more I forgave him, the worse he became. On more than one occasion, he came in around 4 a.m. I was asleep. He tiptoed up the steps and smacked me in the face as hard as he could. I jumped up startled, not knowing what was going on.

Bill screamed in my ear. "Get up and fix me my food…!"

Angry and practically seeing stars, my reply was, "Can you please fix it yourself? I have to get up in a couple of hours and go to work. Why did you smack me?"

Sometimes he gave me so-called reasons and sometimes he didn't. There was no doubt in my mind drugs caused him to act in this manner. On the other hand, maybe it was the angst of withdrawal from not having drugs.

On occasions, if I didn't move out of the bed fast enough, Bill would pull on my legs and virtually drag me down the steps and into the kitchen. I would do whatever he asked of me just to calm him down and try to go back to bed.

Settling for a sandwich late at night was rare. Most of the time, he wanted a full-course meal and nothing less. Whenever I fixed his plate, he would make me taste everything before he ate it. Somebody in his past must have tried to poison him before, I reasoned.

After fulfilling my duties, I thought he would allow me to go back to bed. That was not happening. He would make me sit with him until he was finished eating. Most of the time, dinner was cooked earlier in the day. Bill made me take it out of the refrigerator, reheat it, and fix his plate. When he wanted to aggravate me, he would claim that it wasn't hot enough and throw the food back into the pot. Then I had to reheat it again.

Late one night, he woke me up to fix him some popcorn. I was tired but did it anyway. After fixing it, he made me stay up while he sat there with a smirk on his face. Heading up the steps was not happening. Bill blocked me. I proceeded in the opposite direction towards the living room door. He ran in front of me and blocked me again. Bill told me not to move. I felt like a hostage.

He looked me in my face and told me to say, "Snuckles." Snuckles was the name of a dummy in a movie with a ventriloquist. I looked at Bill as if he was crazy.

Bill said, "I said, say Snuckles."

I refused, so he smacked me. This went on repeatedly while trying to ignore his obnoxious behavior. He then smacked me so hard that I fell backwards into the wooden table. He picked me up, pushed me against the wall, and stuck his elbow in my chest. Then he took his hands, forced my head from side to side, and started cussing me out. I began to weep tremendously.

"I'm only goin' tell you this one more time! Say Snuckles!"Bill said.

Softly, I said, "Snuckles."

Bill said, "Louder!" He was tripping.

"Snuckles!" I said it a little louder.

Bill chuckled, "Whatever way I tell you to turn, you better turn and say Snuckles."

"Turn to your left," said Bill.

I turned to my left and said, "Snuckles."

"Now turn to your right," said Bill.

I turned to my right and said, "Snuckles."

He forced me do this about ten to fifteen minutes, which seemed like eternity. When he was satisfied, he pushed me back up the stairs to bed.

Bill humiliated me to no end. While lying in bed, the tears seem to flow endlessly. The man that I gave my "all and all" to tormented and drained me both emotionally and physically. I didn't know which way to turn. There were times a nervous breakdown felt imminent. I was too embarrassed to tell anyone how much he tormented me. People would think I was crazy for allowing these things to happen. They would never understand. I didn't even understand why I allowed such things to continue to go on. If it was someone else in the same predicament as me, my perception of them would be that they were nuts.

Bill refused to leave me alone. Many times, he would throw rocks at my window and call my name. "Hey Sarah, open the window."

I pretended not to hear him. Bill would begin to sing a song called, "You Are So Beautiful." He would change the word beautiful to wonderful and start the whole song all over again.

If only he were sincere and change for the better. Instead, he seemed like a "wolf in sheep's clothing." Numerous times, I surrendered and opened the door because of my love for him. Other times, it was because of fear of what might happen if I didn't. It was the most difficult situation to have ever experienced.

One day, Bill came to the house. He was in tears.

"What's wrong, Bill?" He began pacing back and forth.

Bill said, "My wife is dead. Somebody done killed my wife!"

Stunned, I said, "Shirley?"

"Yea, and whoever did this is is gonna pay! I'm gonna kill him if the police don't catch him first!"

"What happened?" I tried my best to console him. Bill rarely talked about her, at least not around me.

Bill sobbed and said, "She done went into the woods wit some trick and got beaten and strangled. I tried to tell her that was goin' happen, but she ain't wanna listen. Now she's gone!"

I met Shirley once when Bill took me to New York. She was tall and kind of hard looking. Her reputation appeared to be one of not hesitating to fight a man, if necessary. Bill probably met his match when they got together. I would guess that her street life had a lot to do with her appearance and the way she behaved.

At my first encounter with Shirley, I was upset with Bill, so he tried to convince her to jump me. My resentment had to do with him leaving me at his brother's house for three hours while Bill spent considerable time with her. His so-called brother tried to talk me into sleeping with him. I flat out refused.

While visiting Bill's hometown, I didn't know anyone within close proximity. Otherwise, I would have left. Tina was with me, and we didn't have anything to eat and were hungry. I was more worried about Tina eating than myself. Bill's Brother didn't offer us anything, not even a cracker. I was very uncomfortable and had every right to be mad at Bill.

Bill's wife died a tragic death. I didn't know what else to say to Bill except to give him my condolence. Then, I put my arms around him and tried to comfort him as much as possible. Those weights that were pulling me down didn't matter at this time. I just wanted to be there for him.

Bill left town and went looking for the man who killed his wife. Fortunately, the police had a suspect, which resulted in an arrest. His wife's parents shipped her remains down south. Bill did not go to the funeral.

After the death of his wife, I didn't see or hear from Bill until two months later. Not knowing what he was doing made me a little uneasy. He should have at least been considerate enough to take the time to call to let me know that he was okay. I thought something had happened to him or that he was in jail.

When he finally came home, he acted wilder than ever. I don't know what happened while he was away, but obviously, something bought about the big change. He didn't seem to care about anything or anybody. I believed he still was grieving over the death of his wife.

That night, Bill glared at me and said, "I hate you, Sarah. If you hadn't tried to keep me down here, I would have been wit my wife and none of this would have happened!"

I looked away from him. Arguing or reasoning with him was unnecessary. He was going through a difficult period, and I understood his pain.

"I'm sorry that you feel this way, and no matter what, I will be here for you. I love you, Bill."

Bill held his head down and sighed, "I know, Sarah. Sorry for blamin' you. It just hurts. We had our problems, but she was my ace. Why this had to happen?"

"I don't know why this happened, but I do know everything is going to be all right. Just give it some time."

Days, weeks, and months went by. Bill didn't seem to have any serenity at all. He was just so irritable. Not knowing what else to do, I persuaded him to go to church. To my surprise, it was easier than I thought.

"Bill, I'm going to church tonight. My parents told me that a revival is going on all this week. I feel like I need to go. Why don't you come with me?"

Bill looked at me very serious and said, "Fo what? The church can't help me."

I persisted. "Well, it can't hurt you either. Besides, I heard the preacher was from your home state. He's well known and been on TV, I don't know how many times."

"What his name?" Bill said.

"Brother Paul Zanderlex. You know, "the singer, he preaches now."

Looking flabbergasted, Bill exclaimed, "That's my cous'."

I paused and wanted to call him a liar and say, If *that's your cousin, I have a twin sister that's a billionaire, been a news anchor, been in movies, has her own magazine, and even a TV show that's rated number one.*

Bill was a habitual liar. To call him on his fabrications meant taking a dangerous step. Questioning what was real or not somewhat robbed me of my sanity. Nonetheless, Bill gave me a glimmer of hope with a promise.

"I'll go to church wit you only cause my cous' is preachin'." He dampened the spark of my smile by adding, "But you already know I ain't believing in no God."

Bill would sometimes blaspheme God. I would get so upset and tell him that something bad was going to happen to him if he didn't stop.

Bill's agreement to go to church pleased me, which made me stay close to him all evening for fear of him changing his mind. I walked on eggshells not wanting to make him mad. We both needed to go.

Bill decided to wear his blue jean leather outfit again. Since this wasn't a Sunday morning service, I wore a blue jean skirt with a black top to match my pumps.

It had been a while since I attended church. As we entered, "Holiness Church of God in Christ," the people greeted us with warm and friendly smiles and handshakes. The ushers directed us to a seat close to the front. Bill insisted that we sit in the back.

I asked Bill, nicely, to take his hat off. He refused. After sitting down, he was quiet throughout the remainder of the service. Most importantly, he was there.

When offering time came, he refused to go around the table. While walking to the table, it felt good to see so many people I hadn't seen in a while. Some whispered in my ear and said, "I'm praying for you."

After the contribution, the choir sang. Mom led two songs. One was "Climbing up the Mountain," and the other one was "Tell the Angels." I really enjoyed those two selections as I stood up and clapped my hands. Bill acted rather sullen.

The time had come for the sermon. Brother Paul preached a great message about forgiveness. Bill seemed to be listening. I couldn't ask for more.

After service, we hung around hoping for the opportunity to speak with his cousin, the preacher. I'd seen him on TV, but this was my first time actually meeting him in person. His silky black and white tie went well with his black suit and white dress shirt. On television, he dressed much differently--usually in a black sequence outfit. He was always a happy person and still looked good with his "jerry curl."

113

Brother Paul smiled and shook Bill's hand and said, "Praise the Lord! How are you?"

Bill said, "Doin' just fine. You know me?"

"I don't believe I do. What is your name?"

"Harry Wilson."

I glanced at Bill because I wasn't used to hearing him use his real name.

"I think we kin. My aunt on my dad's side is supposed to be your cousin which makes us cousins." Bill started naming relatives that the preacher never heard of.

Brother Paul Zanderlex said, "I don't recall any of those names, but I'm glad to have met you. Will you be coming back this week?"

Bill was a little disappointed that the preacher didn't own up to being his cousin. Therefore, he wouldn't make any promises.

As Bill walked away, Brother Paul said, "God bless you, man. Jesus loves you."

Bill must have believed, for whatever reason, that they were really cousins. I wasn't much concerned as to whether he lied or not. The fact that he went to church was good enough for me. Bill's mother, Mrs. Jenny Wilson, would be coming to visit soon, and I couldn't wait to tell her.

CHAPTER FIFTEEN

BILL'S MOM WAS ONE OF THE SWEETEST persons I knew. We met on one of my visits to New York with Bill. Our paths didn't cross that often, but when it did, she was nothing but kind to me and my children. Tina and Alisha loved the attention they received from her.

I didn't like the way Bill talked to his mother. When she would come here for a visit, if Bill mistreated me in front of her, she would stick up for me and get on his case.

Bill would tell his mom, "Shut up, you in my house now. You don't like the way I treat my woman, get out, and don't come back!"

I felt so bad and shocked that his mother allowed him to talk to her that way. Bill was so disrespectful. If I said those words to my mother, she would have gone upside my head.

Momma always said, *I bought you into this world, and I'll take you out of this world.*

Mrs. Wilson, along with her daughter, Dianne, claimed me as their favorite out of all the women Bill dealt with. They also met Donna and treated her with respect. However, they couldn't seem to understand how Donna and I associated with each other.

Bill told me numerous times that she was nothing other than a good friend. Donna said the same about Bill. I didn't know what to believe. When we were in the bar together, Bill would make me sit on one side of him and have her on the other. The situation was so bizarre. Because of this, many guys envied Bill. The jealous ones called Donna and I stupid fool's.

Normally, a situation such as this one would cause much hostility. Instead, we got along fine with or without Bill. However, it really bothered me when Bill would purposely pick a fight with me while we were out and then send me home in a "jitney." I believe he planned it that way, so he could spend more time with Donna.

One evening, my sister, Lorraine, was standing on my porch waiting for me. When I got out of the "jitney," Lorraine noticed my countenance and sensed that something was wrong.

She said, "Are you okay?"

"Yeah, why?" I proceeded to enter my home while Lorraine followed me and pretended as if everything was fine.

Lorraine said, "Mom and dad have been calling you but haven't been able to reach you. They're worried about you. Every since you got your own place, you hardly ever come around."

I lied and said, "I probably forgot to turn the ringer back on. Sometimes I turn it off when I get in the bed." I wouldn't dare tell her that Bill was the culprit in unplugging the phone or turning the ringer off. She would have told mom and dad, and they would have begun to worry.

"Well, you need to give them a call to ease their minds," Lorraine said.

"Tell them I'm fine and I'll give them a call tomorrow."

Lorraine sat on the couch. Out of nowhere she blurted out, "I heard that Bill beats you up all the time. I hope that's not true."

I got defensive. "That's not true. We argue a lot just like any couple, but that's about it."

Lorraine looked at me with disbelief. "Your bed is still at the 'crib' and you know you can come back whenever you're ready. Besides, I miss pushing Tina on the swings in the back yard."

"Thanks for your concern, but everything really is just fine." I could feel myself starting to get an attitude and was hoping Lorraine didn't push the issue.

Lorraine was on her way out the door and suddenly turned around. "Sarah, do you mind if I bring Dan over your house on Friday night? You know that's mom and dad's church night. Can you believe I'm still not allowed to have company when they're not home?"

I smiled at Lorraine and said, "Of course you can, but I know what the real reason is. You don't want mom coming home babysitting you." We both chuckled.

After Lorraine left, I made a ham sandwich and turned on the TV to watch the "Jordan Show." Before it went off, I fell sound asleep on the couch.

A loud knock on the door awakened me. Being extremely tired was an excuse for me not to budge. After a minute or so, I heard some keys, which caused me sit straight up. The doorknob turned and in came Bill. He was "high."

I was upset, but remained calm for fear of him attacking me. "When did you get a key to my house, Bill?" It had been two months since the locks were changed.

"Don't worry bout it!" Bill was a little agitated and paced the floor. Trying to make small conversation with him did not help.

"Bill, do you want me to fix you something to eat? I can cut up some potatoes for French fries and fry you some fresh fish. It won't take long." I was tired but had to do something and quick.

With anger in his eyes he said, "Naw, I ain't hungry!"

"Okay. Well, do you want to watch a movie with me then? You can choose something." I handed him the remote, and he threw it against the wall.

I stood up. My mind went blank while trying to think what was wrong this time. I began to feel the pressures of being unable to escape from hell. Gravity seemed to pull me in.

This was the true beginning of the turning point of my life. I couldn't take it any longer. I tried to be home as little as possible mostly by visiting my brother or parent's house more often. I began sharing some things with Lorraine.

Lorraine had just given birth to a beautiful baby girl, named Dorothy Mae. Our daughters were five months apart. My gift to her was the purchase of a playpen. The baby's grandparents on both sides bought everything else she needed.

Dorothy Mae grew just as fast as Alisha did. Lorraine was offended when I said her baby girl looked like a little tweedy bird cartoon character. Apologizing to her came later. I was wrong for making that comment.

Since that day, off and on, we had childish, silly arguments that sometimes resulted in us not speaking to each other for almost a month. Needing a babysitter gave me a reason to break the ice.

I finally was able to purchase a couple pieces of new furniture, a waterbed, and a water couch. The sale price was unbelievably cheap. The company truck planned to deliver at noon, and fill the bed and couch with water. The kids needed to be out of the way. Lorraine agreed to babysit.

About a month later, Bill came home picking an argument over practically nothing. Tina was on her rocking horse and playing in her bedroom upstairs. Alisha was in the living room with me in her playpen. I reached down to pick her up, realizing seconds later that was a big mistake. Bill caught me off guard as he snatched Alisha out of my arms and threw her across the room. She landed on the water couch screaming at the top of her lungs. Trying to get to her was next to impossible, which made me scream for help. Tina hysterically came running down the steps.

"Mommy, mommy, what's wrong?"

Bill blocked the living room entrance and said, "Go back upstairs. Aint nothin' wrong wit yo mammy."

Tina stood there crying while I pleaded with Bill to let me get the baby. Alisha was screaming uncontrollably.

I yelled, "Tina, run out the back door. Go down Mark's and tell him to call the police!" I didn't care what Bill did to me at that point. I wanted my baby and wanted her safe.

Tina ran, but Bill stopped her before she got to the back door. It was perfect timing for me to grab and hold Alisha. While I comforted her, Bill tried to convince Tina that everything was all right.

Bill calmed down and said, "Tina, I'm sorry. Your mom and I had a disagreement. It's okay now."

With a sad face, Tina said, "Then why was Alisha crying?" She demanded an immediate answer.

"Cause, I wouldn't let your momma hold her till I finished talkin'. We tryin' to work things out so we can be one big happy family."

Tina came running into the living room and said, "Mommy, you okay?"

I reassured her and said, "Yes, and the baby's fine. She just needs a bottle. Can you get me a bottle out of the refrigerator and put it in the bottle warmer?" I was glad Alisha had finally calmed down.

Tina said, "Yes, mommy." She went into the kitchen to get the bottle.

"Bill, why would you throw her? She could've got seriously hurt!"

Bill replied, "Oh, well, what I care."

Harshly, I looked at Bill and screamed, "Get out! Get out now!" I was always protective of my kids, and this time he went too far. You could mess with me but not my kids. They were innocent and had nothing to do with our problems.

Tina ran back into the living room with the bottle and sat next to me. She laid her head on my arm. Bill glared at me without any remorse.

Firmly, I said, "Leave now!"

Bill snapped at me and left. I jumped up, locked the screens, the doors, and the windows. Afterwards, I went on a massive search looking for any of his belongings and set everything on the porch in garbage bags.

I called Donna. "Can you please come and get Bill's clothes? They are on the porch in bags."

Donna said, "Why? What's going on?"

"All I'm going to say is that Bill is no longer welcome here. Are you coming or not?"

Donna said, "I'll go out now and see if I can get a ride. I hope everything's okay."

Without responding or saying goodbye, I hung the phone up. Fifteen minutes later, there was a knock on the door.

"Sarah, it's me, Donna, open the door." I refused to answer, so she picked up the bags and left.

Knowing what Bill was capable of doing made me realize more than ever to get him completely out of my life. I should have left him alone a long time ago. Being with him was just a waste of time and energy.

The police were even tired of coming to the "same song and dance." There were times they didn't bother to come at all. That wasn't good.

My life needed a complete change. As far as I was concerned, Bill was not my man anymore. From this day on, I will consider myself a single woman.

CHAPTER SIXTEEN

I MADE A TRIP TO THE A&R Grocery store to purchase several items needed for the house. My list consisted mostly of breakfast and lunch items, but included cleaning supplies and personal items, as well. It didn't take me long to find the items and place them in the shopping cart. While on my way to the checkout line, I grabbed a few snacks for the kids. Ice cream, chips, and cookies were more than enough munchies.

There was a guy in line standing right behind me. As the cashier waited on me, he said, "Lovely day isn't it?"

I turned around and said, "It's a beautiful day. I wish I didn't have to go to work."

He asked, "Where do you work?"

"At the Baker's Steel Mill." I paid for my items and ended the short conversation by saying, "Have a nice day."

By the time I got to my vehicle and unlocked the door, there was a tap on my shoulder. "Miss, you left your bread." I turned around, and saw the same guy I just spoke with in the store.

I thanked him and chuckled. "This was the main reason I went to the store in the first place. I'm so glad I didn't make it home and then have to come back."

He asked, "May I help you put your bags in the van?"

"That's very nice of you. Thank you." His mannerism was impressive.

After he helped me, he put his hand out to shake mine. "By the way, my name is Sherman Smithfield."

I shook his hand and said, "My name is Sarah Jones. Pleased to meet you."

Sherman was dark skinned and roughly six feet tall. He was rather handsome, and had a deep voice, which I admired. As we talked for a few more minutes, he informed me that he was visiting some friends, and lived about an hour away.

I asked, "What do you do for a living?"

He replied by stating he was a sales representative. "I have to go and make a sale now. Do you think we could get together and have coffee sometime?"

"Sure, why not?" It felt good to know that somebody other than Bill might be interested in me. We exchanged phone numbers and stayed in touch.

My way of thinking was not to be in another relationship so soon. A companion was all I ever wanted, and he seemed to be "at the right place at the right time."

After several conversations via phone, we met at the "Jabezza Coffee House" located downtown. I had heard about the place but never been there. When we arrived, I was somewhat puzzled. The environment wasn't what I expected. The people who came in and out appeared to be homeless. This must have been a shelter, which made me feel compelled to hold tightly to my purse.

By the time we left, I knew there would be no returning unless I was on a mission to feed the homeless and those in need. The next time we meet for coffee, my thoughts were to invite him to my house. I felt comfortable with this decision and let Simmone know about my new friend for safety measures.

So far, Sherman seemed very respectful. He was informed about my ex, and assured me that Bill would not bother me as long as he was around.

In a matter of weeks, Bill found out about Sherman. I think the neighbors across the street told him that another man had been coming in and out of my house.

One day, Sherman and I were sitting on the couch watching television and all of a sudden, Bill stuck his head through the living room window.

Bill looked directly at Sherman. "What … are you doin' in my house?" Before anyone could respond, Bill said, "Get out!"

I stood up and practically froze in my steps.

Sherman stuck his chest out and said, "Man, you better go head. She's not your woman anymore, and as long she wants me here, I'm staying!"

That comment sent a spark off in Bill. He swiftly ran to the back door. He broke through and entered the house carrying a sawed-off shotgun. I screamed and ran out the front door. Bill caught me in the middle of the street. His demeanor was obnoxious with rage as he started to hit me with the rifle. Miraculously, a car came up the road and Bill fled.

Sherman came outside and urged me to go into the house. "Are you okay?"

I was a little shaken up. "Yes, but I think you should leave now. I'm getting ready to call the police. We'll talk later."

Sherman didn't waste any time leaving. By the time the police came, Bill was nowhere in sight--neither was Sherman. The police wrote a report.

The police said, "You need to go to the magistrate's office to press charges."

"I will. Thank you, officer."

I didn't take the request and urgency by the police lightly. I went to the magistrate's office the next day and gave them Donnas' mailing address. They scheduled a hearing for us in the middle of July. During those ten days of waiting, fear set in. My final decision was not to show up. The court billed me for the dropped charges.

I went to my brother for help. "Mark, I should've come to you sooner. Do you have time to change my locks?"

Mark said, "It's Bill isn't it?"

"Yes, and I just don't feel safe in my house, anymore."

"You need to leave him alone," Mark said. "He's not doing anything for you."

"I have left him alone." Mark looked at me with disbelief.

The hardware store had just what we needed. My brother did his usual mumbling but changed my locks. I insisted that he nail all my windows shut on the bottom floor as well as the inside frame on the back door. For added protection, a long metal bar wedged between the door and the steps. I felt like a prisoner, but at least Bill couldn't break in.

Linda Foster

Mark said, "I hope you don't have me doing all this work and then you turn around and let him back in."

"That's not going to happen; we're done."

"If you say so. Well, I have to leave now. I need to get to the store before closing time and play my numbers. I feel like I got a hot number."

"Thanks Mark. I hope you hit big time."

After he left, I sat down and really began to reflect. I should have never left my parents' home, which was my safe haven. Now, I have to live with the careless choices made.

Bill was furious about my keeping company with another man. In his eyesight, the betrayal was unacceptable. The double standard was evident.

A concerned person finally informed me that Bill watches my house. Sometimes, he would hide in the back and sometimes in between the houses. Frequently, he caught me off guard and scared the heck out of me.

"I love you girl, and if I can't have you, nobody else will," Bill stated with authority and vengeance.

Refraining Sherman from visiting me had to be done right away. After that, everything remained quiet for a couple of months.

Bill didn't stalk me anymore. I hadn't seen him, and he didn't call. Thinking that he had left town made me feel comfortable enough to have Sherman resume his visits. The thought didn't cross my mind to lock the door when my company arrived. Unfortunately, my guard was let down too soon.

One of my favorite series, "Walking to Your Destiny," was on television. Within forty minutes of Sherman and I getting into the show, Bill walked in the front door with a metal pipe in his hand this time.

He walked directly to Sherman and said, "Ain't I done told you to stay out my house...!"

Sherman stood up to defend himself but didn't have much of a chance. Instantly, Bill started hitting him across the stomach and chest with the metal pipe.

I screamed, "Stop!"

Jumping on Bill's back was the only thing left for me to do. He threw me off like a rag doll. Running to the back door was not an option. It had been nailed shut, which made it impossible for me to escape. That was bad timing on my part. In order for me to flee out the front door, I had to get pass Bill. He stood there glaring at me while holding the pipe.

"Your next!" Bill warned.

The mental torture was seeing Sherman moaning, groaning, and staggering because of me. While holding his stomach, he limped out the door. Bill left behind him cussing up a storm.

Sherman never returned to see me after that episode. On numerous occasions, I tried to reach him by leaving messages on his answering machine. He would not return my calls. Weeks later, someone told me that he had been in the hospital for a while but was doing better.

Bill made it difficult for me to get any new male friends because of his reputation of being wild, crazy, and possessive. The word spread quickly concerning the incident with Sherman. After Bill did all that damage, he attempted once again to get me back.

I was leaving my job, and Bill met me at the gate. "What up!"

"Hi, Bill." I kept walking.

"How was yo day at work?"

I ignored him. My co-worker, Debbie's fiancé, waited for us outside the gate. I quickly got into the back of the vehicle. Driving away with Bill standing there made him look like a fool. That's exactly how I used to feel when Bill embarrassed or played me.

Just the other day, I hid my van in Debbie's garage, so that Bill wouldn't find it. Two days later, Bill was coming out of the post office while I was going in to purchase some stamps.

"Hey 'babe,' you lookin' gorgeous today."

I looked at him disgustingly and was not in the mood to hear the nonsense.

"Can I see the kids later?" Bill asked.

"Sorry, they will be spending the day at their grandma's house."

"Well, how bout tomorrow?" Bill persisted.

Just the sight of Bill got on my nerves. "Tomorrow is a bad day. They have to get their doctor's checkup, and after that, I'll be a little busy."

"Doin' what?"

I looked at him and started to say none of your business. Instead, I lied and said, "I'll be helping mom to do some spring cleaning."

Bill was getting frustrated, but yet trying to be cool. "Well, how bout the movies this weekend?"

"Sorry, I have to work." I had an excuse for everything.

Frustrated Bill said, "Well, when you goin' be free?"

"I don't know. If and when I'm free, I'll let Donna know."

Bill held his peace as he gritted his teeth. Then he reached into his pocket and pulled out a letter. "Please read dis when you get a chance."

I accepted the letter, walked away, and waited until midnight to read it when everyone was sound asleep.

Dear Sarah,

I hope you take time to read this letter; cause there's a lot that I wanna say to you. I admit the way I handle things ain't cool which is enough to make you turn your back on me. As you read this letter, please let your mind and heart open a bit. If you do, try to understand how I'm feelin'. Maybe I might seem to go off a little, but what you doin' ain't helpin' matters no better. If you get one better than me, I could get wit that. I went to the hospital to get my head right for you. I'm gonna leave Donna alone as well as the drugs. Want to show you how much you mean to me. I was hurt so bad. Don't know if you did that to make me jealous or just to show me you don't want me no more. Whatever, you ain't gotta lie. You really touchin' me in a way I'nt been touched before. It's getting to me. Don't want no trouble, but will hurt someone over you and I think you know that. Now I'm willin' to let the past be the past if you want to make up your mind bout forgivin' me. I'm very unhappy bout what I heard. People tellin' me you talkin' to Sherman and it did somethin' to me and you told me that you ain't talkin to no man. I got jealous, and if that was your plan, you did a good job. That boy has a worse habit than me and I ain't sitten' round knowing what could happen to you and not do nothin'. Even though you broke my heart, I'm sure I broke yours too. Sorry. If you give me another chance, I will make it up to you, Smiley. I'm willin' to go along wit what you want just to make things better. Don't wanna lose you, Princes. If you ain't goin' forgive me, please take time to think bout what you getting' into. I know I can't pick your man for you, but if you feel you gotta have one, please get a man not on dope. You already been through that. Don't want no one else to hurt you cause I hurt you enough myself. Right now, I'm hurtin' on the inside. I knew that one day you would kick me so hard, I would finally wake up. I'm tryin' not to do dumb things. I love my kids, and don't want to push you out my life any more. You know I don't usually write letters, but I had to cause I love you and wanna let you know I'm ready to settle down. I deeply miss you. Please take time to read this letter over again and don't tear it up. Be careful hangin' wit Sherman even though he might seem nice.

Bill

I tore the letter up and threw it into the wastebasket. With my hands on my forehead, his words echoed in my head.

A week later, there was an unexpected knock at the door. While peeking out the window, I noticed a white van outside from the "Boaz Floral Shop." The deliveryman was at the door holding the most beautiful roses.

I opened the door and accepted the flowers, which included an attached card.

It read, *Sarah, please forgive me. I was wrong. I'm sorry. Give me another chance. Love, Bill.*

The flowers were not from Sherman as I had hoped, so the bouquet went into the wastebasket.

Tina said, "Mommy, who gave you dose flowers?"

"Oh, nobody important."

Tina had a serious look on her face. "Well, why you throw em in the garbage?"

"Because I don't have time to take good care of them." Changing the subject was the best thing for me to do before she asked me any more questions.

"How about us ordering some pizza for dinner?"

Tina said, "Ooh, thank you, mommy. Can we get extra cheese and pepperoni?"

"Of course," I said. "Jermaisha's Pizza House" was the first place in mind. They had good pizza. I grabbed the phone book to look for the number, and called. The special included two toppings. Delivery service was available, and the waiting time would be about 25 minutes.

In the meantime, Alisha received her bath and had her bottle. She fought sleep while lying in the playpen.

The cheesy and delicious hot pizza came in no time. The aroma filled the whole house. After eating two slices, Tina had a full belly. Three pieces filled me up. We put the rest in the refrigerator for the next day.

Tina and I took our baths before sitting on the water couch to watch television. Cartoons were on. One of my favorite shows, "It's Not What It Looks Like," came on next. The show was hilarious.

Tina fell asleep, which gave me a little quiet time to enjoy the moment when "The Dance Mobile" came on. I was nowhere close to mimicking the way they moved. My expertise was certainly not in dancing but no one was watching, so it didn't matter. Dancing the entire hour of the show tired me out.

Alisha didn't budge as I placed her in the crib. Carrying Tina up the steps, after being so tired, was a little too much. I nearly dropped her.

The night had ended and I said my prayers while getting in my comfortable bed.

Right before encountering a trip to "la la land," someone was singing outside my window. It was Bill. He got louder and louder. I never heard that song before. I think he made it up. His vocal chords needed a tune-up, and I only wished he'd shut up. Closing the window gave me hope for some relief, which only gave him the initiative to sing even louder. Bill sounded like a "croaking frog."

When he realized his singing was in vain, he slowly started walking away, and the noise began fading. The corner of the curtain gave me just enough light to see Bill as he repeatedly turned around. After that, he was gone. The next morning there was a letter in my door. Before opening it, I knew it was from Bill.

Dear Sarah,

If you only knew the love, I have for you. Hey girl, let me tell you what's been goin' thru my mind. It's a serious love we can share together. I constantly am thinkin' of you, and I'm tryin' to prove to you what you mean to me. I don't want to mess over you no more. We got a baby we love very much. I'm just gonna try to be the man you want me to be. You mean the world to me and my wishes are to bring you all the joy you brought to me. I wish to make your fondest dreams come true. I'm so in love wit you and you are a special part of my life. Please try to get wit me. Okay, you win. I wanna be your husband, please. I need you and love you so much. It seems there ain't enough days in a lifetime wit you, and not enough ways to show you I care. I'll be waitin' for you, no matter how long it takes. Please marry me. I love you, Sarah."
From Bill

After reading that letter, my emotions were like a roller coaster again. After reading it numerous times, I placed it in my drawer.

Bill just simply refused to stop pursuing me. He thought up another excuse to be around by asking me to go to church with him. Now that was a big extraordinary change.

Bill called me on the phone. "Sarah, I'm ready to change my life. Will you go wit me to church this Sunday?"

There was a moment of silence. I really wanted to believe in him. My grandmother had instilled in me that there was a little good in everybody. She said it takes a strong-willed person to see it. Going to church was a good thing. I hope he had the right motive.

"Bill, you can go to church, but I'm not going with you."

If the sincerity were there, he would go regardless. Bill mumbled something, and I hung the phone up on him. My phone rang again. I did not answer. Bill never made it to church.

He left a message on the answering machine. "Pick up the phone, Sarah. I know you hear me. Why you keep treatin' me like this? You know I love you. Well, when you ready, give me a buzz."

I didn't return that call. The relationship just wasn't the same. My focus needed to be more on my kids and getting myself together. Alisha's birthday was coming up, and I planned to throw her a party.

CHAPTER SEVENTEEN

THE SECOND OF NOVEMBER WAS THE date for Alisha's birthday party. An invitation went out to about twenty to thirty children--mostly family members.

My two best friends, Jannetta and Simmone, received an invitation even though we weren't as close as we used to be. I avoided them a lot because Bill never allowed me to have any close friends unless it was his choice. Not wanting to know how they truly felt about my relationship with Bill, also kept me away. Explaining things or confided in them, might give them the impression I was a fool just as everybody else thought.

Two days before the party, Bill called. "Hey 'babe', I heard you throwin' a birthday party on Saturday for our daughter. Why ain't you told me?"

"I haven't had the time to go looking for you, that's why."

Bill asked, "Did you order the cake yet?"

"Yes, I did."

"You need help wit food?" Bill asked.

'Thanks, but no thanks."

Persistent Bill asked, "You have help wit the kids?"

I said, "Lorraine and some of the other parents will be there to help me."

Bill began to get a little edgy. "Well, am I invited or not?"

"As long as you don't come here high, or start any trouble, you are welcomed to come."

Bill had not been violent with me since Sherman was out of the picture. Not allowing him to spend time with our daughter on her birthday would have been morally wrong.

Bill seemed offended. "Oh, now, come on, you ain't gotta go there. I know how to behave at my daughter's birthday party."

The cool temperature on the day of the party went down to roughly fifty degrees. The celebration would start at 4 p.m. Bill came unexpectedly at 12 noon.

"Came early to help out. Hope you don't mind."

"I guess it would be all right. Come on in." I was in the middle of decorating, so Bill pitched right in to help me. Streamers needed taped to the walls. Bill blew up all the balloons and found places for them to stick. The colorful and huge happy birthday sign placed on the entrance to the living room was the last of the decorations.

Bill took it upon himself to grab the sweeper and vacuum all the rugs. While he did that, I cleaned the kitchen and placed a red plastic tablecloth on the dining room table. I was grateful for Bill's help.

The pickup time for the birthday cake was 2 p.m. When everything else was ready, we went to my parent's house to get the kids. They had been anxiously waiting for me since 10 a.m. Bill remained in the car. Lorraine, unexpectedly, came out with the girls.

The moment Lorraine saw Bill; she walked over to the vehicle and sarcastically said, "Well, well, well, look what we have here!" She pretended to tip a hat. "How do you do, sir?"

Bill snapped back as he got out of the van. "Well, well, well, looks like you need a meal. Howdy, Madam."

Lorraine was certainly not afraid of Bill. "You've got a lot of nerve with your wild west cowboy-looking hat and boot self. Looks like you need a snag!" A snag was another name for dope.

Bill would not let up. "As bony as you are, look like you had a snag!"

Lorraine leaped at Bill while I got between them. "That's why your face is so sunk in, you old monkey-looking face werewolf." Lorraine was furious.

Bill laughed.

I interrupted their little spat and reminded them both that today is Alisha's birthday. I pleaded with them not to spoil her party.

Lorraine had an attitude. "Sarah, I think it's best for me come down a little later."

I begged, "Oh, please don't do this to me. You need to pick out some games to play from the party book. I don't have time to do that because I have to take a shower and get dressed."

Lorraine rolled her eyes at Bill. "Okay, if you really need me."

Lorraine and Bill ignored each other the rest of the day. As long as they were not arguing, I could deal with that.

The party turned out nice and we sang "Happy Birthday." Alisha received many gifts, and Bill didn't give me any problems. I couldn't ask for more.

Lorraine caught a ride home with Mark, and I dropped Bill off at the bar. The day was long, and he seemed anxious to get high. Anyway, I had enough of him for one day.

A few days later, Jerry drove pass me. While I was on my way to visit my friend, Jannetta, he stopped when he noticed me getting out of the van. He beckoned me to get into his vehicle, and we went for a ride.

Jerry said, "What's happening? I haven't heard from you in a while."

"I've been around. I've just not been hanging in the bar as much as I used to. I've been having too many problems with Bill."

"I heard what happened to Sherman," Jerry said.

"Yeah, Bill was acting really crazy for a while. We're not together, but he still doesn't want me seeing other men."

Jerry said, "Of course not. He knows he had a good thing going on, and he blew it, that's why."

"I really tried, Jerry. I wanted it to work. I've bent over backwards and forwards for him. I've done things that I've never done before just to please him. I feel like there's nothing left in me to try again."

"I hear you, but what are you going to do about resolving the whole matter?"

"I honestly don't know. I really wish he would just leave town for good. It would be so much easier for me not to give in to his manipulations. I want my children and me to have a good life. I desire to have new furniture, new clothes, and the whole nine yards. I just can't seem to get ahead with Bill around."

Jerry asked, "Well, do you still love him?"

"You just had to go there, didn't you?" Jerry smiled while waiting for me to answer.

"Truthfully, I don't know how I feel anymore. He's certainly done enough to me to change the love that I once had."

Jerry said, "You love him."

"I didn't say that."

"You don't have to."

I changed the subject, and we started talking about some problems going on with my van. After riding around for about an hour, Jerry dropped me off on Park Avenue close to my vehicle. He reached over to shake my hand and handed me a $100 bill. I was surprised.

"You and the kids have dinner on me." Jerry smiled and drove off.

I stood there waving as he drove off. He watched me through the rear view mirror.

"Thank you!" The conversation and the ride were very enjoyable. From that day on, we became very close. Unfortunately, he was married.

Bill had originally introduced me to Jerry. Selling cocaine for Jerry was how it all started after which he became my main supplier. Bill seemed to be a little jealous whenever he saw us talking.

After seeing us together so frequently, Bill accused me of having an affair. He was wrong. Jerry had a lot of respect for me. He never tried to take advantage of our friendship. When we were together, it was just business.

Jerry was a major drug dealer. He had the reputation of being very powerful with many connections. Everyone respected him, and he was a good person. He always helped people in need. Anytime I wanted something, he was there for me. The closer we became, the more Jerry wanted to protect me, and the more I began to trust him.

The next time Jerry and I were together, he said, "I keep hearing a lot of negative things concerning you. Is Bill still bothering you?"

"He hasn't put his hands on me in a while, but he keeps threatening me. Somebody keeps telling him that we are messing around. I told him that it's not true and we're nothing but friends. He doesn't believe me."

With a serious look on his face, Jerry said, "I don't care what he believes. All I know is that he better not put his hands on you anymore." His remark surprised me.

"If you are really serious about leaving Bill alone, I will pay a lawyer for you to get a "Protection Against Cruelty Order." If you're not serious, I think we should stop seeing each other on a personal level. I don't need any kind of problems that might interfere with my business. It's too risky. I have heard that you went through this before and didn't show up at the hearing. Now what do you want to do?"

I thought for a minute. "I think I'll take you up on that because I know you can't always be around to protect me." That was very thoughtful of him to offer.

"Then it's settled!" Days later, Jerry made phone calls and did what he had to do. He made an appointment for me to meet with a lawyer. After questioning me, the lawyer drew up a temporary "Protection Against Cruelty Court Order." The instructions were for me to take the papers to the police station so they could hand deliver a copy to Bill.

The scheduled court date was August 29, 1981, at 9 a.m. The hearing would be in the courtroom of Judge Peytonfield on the fourth floor of the Criminal Justice Building. When filing the papers, I wrote down his alias name, William Taylor. I was afraid to tell the authorities his real name because of his previous threats made to me.

Prior to the court date, I didn't see or hear from Bill. My gut feeling told me that he was up to something. The unknowing made me very tense. Several times, in the wee hours of the night, I heard noises, which interfered with my sleep. The kids, along with my telephone were in the bed with me.

I couldn't wait for the final court papers to come. This would prevent Bill from coming in or around my house for a period of one year.

Finally, the day came for our hearing. Bill showed up with his Uncle Jason. His arrival time was approximately 8:50 a.m. My attorney, Thomas Jatah, met with me at 8:30 a.m. Since he was well known and recommended by Jerry, I felt confident of him representing me. We discussed a few things while waiting. The court had quite a few cases before us.

The Tipstaff said, "All rise." We swore in around 10:45 a.m.

Judge Peytonfield read the petition. After carefully reading it aloud, he looked at Bill and asked, "Is this true?"

"No, man, I mean your honor. I ain't done those things that I'm accused of. I ain't never threatened her either. She's lying!"

Judge Peytonfield said, "The petitioner is stating that you frequently abused her. She has hospital records stating that you came in the hospital and punched her in the mouth. She is also stating that you threatened to do bodily harm to her on numerous occasions."

"Your honor, I say some things, but she knows I ain't mean it, and when I went to the hospital, I was 'swoll,' cause I thought she was tryin' to get rid of our baby. I love her, your honor. I would never do nothin' to hurt her. She's my baby's momma!"

"I don't care how angry you were. That still doesn't give you the right to hit her." Judge Peytonfield said.

Bill said, "The only reason she down here in the first place is cause of big-head Jerry Caldwell."

Judge Peytonfield said, "And what does he have to do with this case?"

"He's a dope dealer and wants my woman, and now he got her makin' up all these lies."

"Does the petitioner wish to have anything to say?"

Attorney Thomas Jatah stood up. "My client, Sarah Jones, is in fear of her life and wishes the honorable judge to grant her a "Protection Against Cruelty Order" that will keep Bill away from her and her premises."

Judge Peytonfield handed down his decision:

And now, to wit, this 29th day of August 1981 after final hearing in the above captioned matter, it is hereby ordered and judged and decreed as follows:

For a period of one year from the date of this order, Respondent must not come near nor enter on the premises of the petitioner.

1) Custody of the minor children of petitioner and respondent is granted to petition.

2) Respondent must not physically abuse petitioner or the minor children.

3) The police having jurisdiction of the petitioner's residence shall enforce this order

4) If Respondent violates this order, he is to be arrested on the charge of indirect criminal contempt. An arrest for violation of this order may be without warrant, based solely on probable cause, whether or not the violation is committed in the presence of the police officer.

5) If Respondent is arrested for violation of this order, he should be taken immediately before this court. If this court is unavailable, he should be taken immediately before a District Justice, and be arraigned and bond is to be set immediately.

6) Respondent is to pay counsel for petitioner $500 in attorney fees.

7) Respondent is to pay court costs.

Court is dismissed.

Bill took one look at me and stormed out of the courtroom shaking his head. I thanked my attorney, who suggested that I wait around in the hall to get the necessary papers. This would give Bill time to be long gone before exiting the building.

Jerry called around 6 p.m. "What's up, Sarah?"

"Hi, Jerry. I've been waiting for your call."

"I was a little tied up earlier, so I'm just getting a chance to call you. How did things go?"

"Well, the case went in my favor, and I was able to get the final "Protection Against Cruelty" court order. Thank you Jerry, but…," I hesitated.

"But what?" Jerry asked.

"Bill told the judge that you were a dope dealer and that you got me making up all of these lies because you wanted his woman."

"I know he didn't say that!" Jerry was angry.

"Yes, he did, and I'm sorry I got you involved. If I had known he was going to say those things about you, I never would have agreed to go."

"Sarah, you did the right thing for your protection. I will deal with Bill when I see him."

"What are you going to do?" I didn't want anything bad to happen to Bill. I only wanted him to stop threatening and abusing me.

"This is not your problem anymore! This is between me and Bill!"

I pleaded, "Please, just let it go. I'm okay and I got my 'Protection Against Cruelty Order.' There's no need to do anything."

I was a little worried. Both of them carried guns. If something happened to either one of them, I would never forgive myself.

Jerry tuned me out and said, "I got to go. I'll rap with you later."

After hanging up the phone, I sat there stunned for a moment. Immediately, I got on my knees to pray:

Lord, I appreciate the
Protection Against Cruelty

Order, but more important, I'm grateful for your everlasting protection for me and my family. And please Lord, let there be peace between Jerry and Bill. I don't want anyone to get hurt. I'm sorry for the problems I've caused. Thank you for hearing my prayer. Amen.

Jerry was worried because the "fuzz" would definitely be watching him now. He had to change his routine completely and lay low--thanks to Bill.

A few days later, I was in the kitchen cooking dinner before picking up the kids. It was about 6:30 in the evening. Because of the intensity of the heat due to the oven being on, I opened the door to get air. Bill didn't want to go to jail, so I was sure he would stay away. The children were at my sister-in-law's house.

All of a sudden, Bill came running in. He hurled accusations and slanders at me, which were totally unfounded. With jealous rage, Bill roared, "I know for a fact you messin' round with Jerry. Admit it!"

Frantically, I answered, "That's not true!"

Bill grabbed me and said, "You lied to me for the last time!" He shoved me to the floor and called me everything but Sarah. I blocked my face and head as he threw an ashtray at me. Then he slammed the front door and locked it. He began throwing me around the living room. I screamed to the top of my lungs. No one came to my rescue, and I was unable to get to the telephone or the door. Bill grabbed me by my hair and pulled me up the steps to the bedroom. I fought back.

For a period of about fourteen hours, Bill put me through hell. He snatched my purse and found the package of cocaine Jerry had just given me. Because of his hateful and jealous attitude, Bill forced me to get high. I had been clean for a while and had no desire to use drugs. He spotted the bottle of Windsor on the dresser and made me drink it straight. The room started spinning. Attempting to get away was impossible as I staggered and fell. Bill kept hitting, punching, and throwing me around. I tried to fight back. Because of my drunken state, I kept swinging but missing his body.

The beatings continued periodically throughout the entire night. The mental abuse was as bad as the physical abuse. Bill made me put on a mini-skirt, bend down, and touch my toes, after which he accused me of trying to be cute. Then he hit me again.

"Stop it! Please!" I begged.

"Shut up…!" Bill yelled. "You asked for this!"

My cries and screams had no benefit. I prayed that Lorraine or Mark would knock on the door. My prayers seem to go unheard.

Without my consent, Bill forced me to have sex with him. He got angrier by the minute, and I became sicker. The pillow that was now in Bill's hands seemed to float in my direction. My hands went up to catch it as he placed it over my face. I fought and kicked with all my might for my life, which seemed to be ending. I felt myself slipping away. Then Bill released the pillow from my face. I was too limp to move.

I started seeing double visions of Bill drinking Windsor and shooting drugs in his arm.

"Stand up. I ain't finish wit you yet," he yelled. I obeyed and slowly wobbled over to him not realizing his next move. He took a can of hairspray and sprayed my hair. He threatened to light it with a torch. My words slurred as I begged him repeatedly not to do it. For some mysterious reason, he put the torch away.

The incident in the bathroom further proved how ruthless he was. He gagged my mouth with a dirty washrag. I started vomiting my guts out. Bill ridiculed me and made me clean it up. I passed out and lay helplessly on the floor. When I came to, Bill was standing over me staring. I honestly don't know what else happened to me while being unconscious.

Being weak and messed up, but alive, gave me a mind to pray silently. Tears were streaming uncontrollably down my face.

Oh God, I've heard dad say that you were an "On-Time" God. He wouldn't have said that unless he knew for himself. Well, here I am standing in need of your help. Come to my rescue. Please make him quit. Please!

I believe God heard me that time. No sooner finishing that prayer, Bill suddenly got tired. Once again, he made me lie down beside him and warned me not to get out of bed. Within ten minutes after raping me again, he was snoring and in a deep sleep. I disobeyed his request.

My body felt like a "ton of bricks." Quietly, I crept out of bed and managed to slip on some clothes grabbing the first pair of shoes within my reach. After getting downstairs, I noticed the two left mix-matched shoes that were on my feet. It didn't matter.

I couldn't find my glasses either; however, it didn't stop me from leaving. Bill had hid my van keys, so driving was impossible. All I needed to do was to make it to my brother's house.

As I staggered down the street looking a mess, people were staring at me and whispering to each other from their porches. My eyes were puffy, my hair stood in every direction, and my clothes didn't match. My right foot hurt from having on a left shoe. I was so embarrassed.

My brother's house was five minutes away. Because of the shape I was in, it took me fifteen to twenty minutes to get there. I knocked and knocked. In about two minutes, my brother answered the door.

He took one look at me and said, "What ... happened to you?"

My appearance was evident that something was going on. I couldn't lie anymore. "Bill did this!"

Mark could not believe what he was seeing. "What?"

"Mark, please don't question me right now. I just need to lie down. I'm so sick."

Mark was upset. "Why in the world did you let him in?" Before answering him, I had to run to the bathroom to vomit again. The straining and gagging took a toll on me because there was no water or food in my system. I barely could catch my breath. My brother looked as if he wanted to cry. My pounding head was in need of a cold rag. Mark gave me one as well as a glass of water. The room seemed to take a spin as I lay on the couch.

After resting for a couple of hours, I managed to pick up the phone and call Jerry. Surprisingly, he answered on the first ring. After telling him what had happened, he advised me to call the police.

The officers came to my brother's house. No details were explained other than the fact that Bill hit me. My appearance was evident.

The police asked, "Why did you let him in?"

"I didn't. He just walked in."

The police arrested Bill and charged him with simple assault and harassment. His bail was set at $1,000@10%. Someone paid it and he was soon out.

When the "Protection Against Cruelty" court hearing came around, two witnesses showed up and stated that I willfully let him in the house. Because of their cunning testimony and lies, he wasn't in violation of the court order.

We still had a hearing scheduled for the simple assault and harassment case. I supposed that they fingerprinted Bill, which would prove his identity. I couldn't understand why they didn't know who he really was.

Jerry waited until the police left the area of my brother's house, and took me to a hotel. "Clean yourself up and just rest," Jerry said. The smell of liquor was coming out of my pores and a shower was crucial to my well-being.

Jerry had checked me into the "Need a Rest Hotel" and walked me to my room. He gave me some money for food and left me to unwind and get some rest. Although I wasn't feeling well, I pushed myself to take a much-needed shower.

Room service was just a phone call away. Chicken noodle was the soup of the day, and that was all I needed. A couple of sips did wonders. Now, I was ready to lie down. The aches and pains in my body made it hard for me to get comfortable. After crying my heart out, I fell into a deep sleep. My uninterrupted sleep lasted about ten hours straight. Upon awakening, my sore body felt a little revived.

I sat up and looked around the extravagant room. The nice plush-brown soft carpet felt good to my feet. The furniture was made of lavish pinewood. The 27-inch screen television had a VCR connected to it. I barely noticed the stereo system inside the entertainment center.

The satin sheets on the bed felt so soothing to my body. To the left was the sitting area, which consisted of a tan leather couch and a coffee table matching the rest of the furniture. The luxurious bathroom complimented the Jacuzzi. The fixtures were made of pure gold. Jerry must have spent a lot of money on this room. It must have been a suite.

A coffee pot was located on the table. Drinking coffee had never been my normal, but anything to make me feel better would do. While the coffee brewed, I turned on the television. Talk shows were on most of the channels. Watching the news would be just fine.

I called room service to order something to eat with my coffee. A slice of toast, a piece of fruit, and some orange juice was sufficient. Finishing breakfast before another warm shower relaxed me even more. Jerry picked me up around 11 a.m.

"Hi Jerry."

Jerry said, "You look so much better. How are you feeling?"

"A whole lot better. I needed the rest. Thank you."

As he was taking me home, he never once brought up Bill's name and neither did I. The rest of the conversation was very short. There was not a lot to say. Something seemed to be on his mind. Jerry took me to pick up my children and then brought us home.

As I was getting out the car, Jerry asked, "Are you sure you're going to be okay?"

"Yeah, I'll be fine. Thank you. I'll talk to you later." I was determined not to involve him with any more of my problems. After going into the house and locking the door, I found my glasses and keys underneath my bed.

Rumors were going around that Jerry ran into Bill the day before and shot at him. I was so glad no one was hurt. Maybe he just wanted to scare him. I heard Bill ducked and fled in a car.

Bill stayed away from me for a while until remembering my birthday. My plans were to be with Jerry hoping that Bill wouldn't find out. I didn't need any more trouble.

CHAPTER EIGHTEEN

MY 25TH BIRTHDAY HAD ARRIVED, AND my intentions were to enjoy the evening. The kids were with mom for the weekend. Jerry and I planned to meet at the bar. I chatted with a few people while waiting patiently.

Jerry strolled in around 9 p.m. and mingled for a few minutes. He then signaled for me to meet him outside. Next, he followed me to my parents' house where I parked my van. His new Lincoln Continental Town car was nice and cozy.

"Happy birthday!" He presented me a card.

I smiled, thanked him, and placed the envelope in my purse. There was no doubt in my mind that there would be money inside that card.

Jerry said, "What time is your curfew?"

I laughed and said, "The same time as yours."

"If you say so."

"Where are we going?" I asked.

"Where do you want to go?"

"I wouldn't mind going to a movie as long as it's not around here." Running into someone that knew us might create some problems.

Jerry smiled and we were on our way. The nice long ride was enjoyable. The breeze, the scenery, and the lights in the city made the night glamorous and peaceful. Jerry pulled over and circled the lot until he found a parking space. This certainly was not the movies. I guess he had different plans. Jerry opened the car door for me, and offered his hand to help me get out.

I asked, "Now, where are you taking me?"

"I have two tickets to go on a boat ride. We will be boarding the "Escape Away Ship" in about thirty minutes to take a tour of the whole city. The boat ride is about two and a half hours."

"Ah, that was so kind of you. You didn't have to do this. I would have been fine just going to a movie." I had never been on a boat ride for a date before and was determined to enjoy the moment.

Jerry said, "I wanted to do this just to show that you deserve better than what you are getting."

We stood in line for about twenty minutes before boarding. A nice crowd of people stood in the midst. I was thankful that no one recognized me.

A "DJ" started out playing oldies but goodies. The music sounded so good that we remained on the dance floor for a considerable amount of time. Jerry's movements tickled me. He was doing the "Jerk" while I attempted to do my usual Penguin dance. I had to give him credit. At least he had a little rhythm.

I said, "I didn't know you could cut a step like that."

It must have gone to his head because he said, "Well, I try."

However, all that dancing forced him to stop to catch his breath. He was huffing and puffing.

"Let's go upstairs to the second floor. The buffet should be ready," said Jerry.

That was fine by me. By now, we had both worked up an appetite. The tasty food on the buffet consisted of fried and baked chicken, baby back ribs, rice pilaf, pork and beans, potato salad, coleslaw, corn on the cob, linguine salad, fresh vegetables with dip, watermelon, and an assortment of desserts. The cash bar sold beverages. A bottle of water was all I wanted to drink. Jerry bought a beer.

The boat ride was wonderful and coming close to an end. We went to the top floor where the atmosphere was extremely peaceful except for the smell of the cigarettes. However, on one side, there seemed to be a little less smoke. We quickly went in that direction, and sat where there was a perfect view of the whole city. The rest of the tour gave us a chance to just relax and talk.

I looked at Jerry and said, "I'm having a great time. This was so nice of you to bring me here."

Jerry said, "I want you to remember this night and may this not be the last time. You deserve the best, and you need to leave those 'knuckleheads' alone that don't know how to respect and treat you good."

That remark made me feel special. I hadn't felt this way in a very long time.

Jerry was my best friend, and I enjoyed every minute of his company. He was trustworthy and the utmost respect was due to him. There was never any physical intimacy--just plain good friendship.

After the boat ride was over, we managed to escape the crowd. On our way home, I thanked Jerry again for such a wonderful time.

Jerry said, "My pleasure!"

He dropped me off at my van. It was somewhat late, and I didn't want to go to my house. Lorraine had my keys. She spent the night with plans for her baby's father to meet her there.

My mom left the screen door unlocked for me. Quietly, I unlocked the other door and tiptoed upstairs. Tina was in my bed with Alisha, so I found a blanket and lay on the floor. Lorraine's baby, Tanya, was in the crib in the spare bedroom sound asleep.

The next morning I woke the kids up early and took them home. Lorraine opened the door. Her facial expression was one of seeing a ghost.

I said, "Good morning. Did your company show up?"

Lorraine said, "Sure did, after Bill left."

She didn't look like she was joking. "What?"

"He broke in your house, and was hiding, waiting for you to come in."

"Oh my God! How did he get in and where was he hiding?"

"I don't know how he got in. All I know is I was here by myself minding my own business. The dining room closet door was cracked. I slammed it shut and then went into the kitchen to pop some popcorn. About five minutes later, all of a sudden, he busted out the closet, sweating like crazy. He scared the crap out of me. He said, I thought Sarah was comin' in tonight. I wanted to surprise her for her birthday."

147

"Surprise me?" I couldn't believe my ears.

"Yea, he said he bought you something for your birthday. There it is over there in that box."

I opened the box.

"He's lying," I stated in unbelief. "He been bought me this negligee."

His conniving plans didn't work. The closet got unbearably hot, and Bill couldn't stay closed in any longer. I don't want to think about what might have happened if I came home instead of Lorraine being there.

Lorraine continued. "His exact words were, 'She can nail those windows, and she can lock those doors, and I still can get in!' He had the look of the devil in his eyes when he spoke."

After that remark, while Bill was still there, Lorraine stated she picked up the phone to call Mark's stepson, Carter. Lorraine whispered, requesting him to come to the house. He didn't seem to comprehend her words. He kept asking her what she said. Bill was standing there, which made Lorraine unable to speak louder. Due to the lateness of the hour, Carter hung up on her not knowing what was going on.

Bill waited around a little while longer hoping that I would soon walk through those doors. Lorraine felt a sigh of relief when he finally left. She locked all the doors and checked the windows. Her baby's father, Dan, showed up afterwards and stayed for the rest of the night.

Bill's plans had backfired and he was angry. The next day he decided to make an unexpected trip to my parents' house. Lorraine had already gone home.

Shortly after, Lorraine called me and said, "Make sure your doors are locked. Do you know Bill just left here?"

"Now what?"

Lorraine said, "Someone knocked on the door. When I opened it, Bill was standing there. He said he wanted to talk to mom. Dad wasn't home, so I told Bill he couldn't come in. He pushed me out of the way, and I pushed him back. Then I noticed he had his hands on his gun, fortunately, he didn't pull it out. I stepped back, and mom came in the room and asked him what he wanted."

"What did he tell her?"

"He told her that you were using and selling drugs and that you were messing around with a married man. He also told her that I'm always having a lot of different men down your house."

I was flabbergasted and said, "No he didn't! What did mom say?"

"She told him to leave. Immediately, Bill left. I guess he knew not to mess with mom."

"Thanks for letting me know."

I was furious. Bill had no right to tell mom our business. Immediately, I called Latisha and asked her to babysit. Without carefully thinking this matter over, I went straight to Donnas' house. As I expected, Bill was there.

I was furious, but fearful of raising my voice, due to numerous accounts of experiencing his wrath.

"Bill, why did you tell my mother all that stuff about Lorraine and me? You had no right."

Bill replied, "Woman, get out my face wit that mess. Don't play stupid wit me. You know exactly why I done it."

"You are so wrong. You know, my mom didn't need to hear that. All the stuff you have done, I have never said anything to your mom."

Bill cussed at me and asked, "Where were you last night? Ain't no since of lying cause someone saw you leave the bar and five minutes later, Jerry left. I know you were wit him."

I had to think quickly so I lied. "I was with Simmone and Jannetta. We went to all-night bowling."

Bill didn't believe me and got ready to hit me.

Donna intervened. "Don't bring that mess in here, I'm not getting evicted because of you two fighting."

Bill stormed out the house. I put my jacket on but decided it was best for me to wait a little while before leaving.

I owed Donna an apology. "Donna, I'm sorry for coming to your house with that mess."

"I don't mind you coming here. You have welcomed me in your house and you're more than welcome in mine. I just didn't want him to jump on you, nor do I want to get put out."

"I was just so upset about what he told my mom."

"Well, what did he say?" Donna was curious.

"He told her that I sold and used drugs and that I was messing with a married man. You know my parents are in the church, and they certainly didn't need to hear that."

"Well, do you think they believed him?"

"I don't know. I haven't talked to my mom since that happened. Right now, I don't want to face her."

Donna stated, "That's a shame. He shouldn't have done that. That was between you and him."

Donna was in the middle of cooking dinner, so she asked me to come into the kitchen while she finished preparing her meal. She made fried chicken, French fries, and a salad. Dinner didn't take very long for her to prepare.

"Why don't you stay and have dinner? You're more than welcome, and I have plenty."

"I think I need to get out of here before Bill comes back."

"Don't worry about Bill. If he was going to do something to you, he would've done it when he was here." She kept assuring me to trust her, and that he was not going to bother me.

"Okay, I'll stay just for a little while. I am hungry. Can I use your phone to check on the kids? They are at my sister-in-law's house."

"Sure, any time you need to use the phone, you know you can."

I called to check on the kids and they were fine.

While I was in the middle of fixing my plate, Bill came back. I put my plate down on the table just in case I had to defend myself. The element of surprise was not going to happen today. I watched his every move. However, Bill ignored me and went straight to the bathroom. The perfect opportunity presented itself for me to leave quietly.

Donna kept assuring me that everything was okay. I trusted her. Ten minutes later, he came out of the bathroom. I looked him straight in the eyes. Blasted Bill had a plate of cocaine in his hand with a little straw in the middle of the dish. He gave it to Donna. She picked up the straw, sniffed a line of cocaine, and then handed it to me.

I declined, "No thanks. I've been doing quite well since I haven't been getting high. I've had too many problems behind that stuff."

Donna didn't say anything. She picked the plate up a second time and sniffed another line of cocaine. As I watched her, temptation started getting the best of me. Leaving would have been the smartest thing to do at that moment.

As Bill ran back and forth to the bathroom, there was a battle going on in my mind. The more Donna sniffed, the weaker my flesh became. She didn't have to persuade me anymore. I just wanted it. The plate was lying on the table in my face.

I couldn't resist it any longer, picked the plate up, made a line, and took a sniff up one of my nostrils. After that, I made another line and took a sniff up the other nostril. We passed the plate to each other several times. The party was on, and it became too hard for me to stop. Bill was watching.

"Sarah, could you come in here for a minute?"

Speechless, I went into the bathroom feeling numb. Bill told me to sit down. Without asking any questions or resisting, I complied. He tied a belt around my arm. After much searching for a vein, the needle was in. My ears began to ring. Any movement was unthinkable.

He left me in the bathroom in a mesmerized stupor. Moments later, he returned with a camera in his hand. Bill snapped a few pictures of me with the needle still in my arm.

Reality of what just happened blew my mind. Conniving Bill set me up. I attempted to speak and tell him off. Instead, the words came out somberly. "Get this needle out of my arm."

With a smirk, Bill took the needle out of my arm. He left me in the bathroom while hiding the camera. I refused to believe that Donna knew he planned a stunt like that. Had I not listened to her about staying for dinner, none of this would have happened.

While sitting there feeling dumb and helpless, the minutes seem to come and go quickly. I couldn't do anything but ride it out. Shortly after, Bill left.

Two hours later, I felt okay enough to go home and pull myself together. My throat was extremely dry. A glass of water was what I needed the most. It tasted strange because my taste buds were off. I didn't have an appetite but forced myself to eat a bowl of hot chicken noodle soup with crackers.

Being angry with Bill was beyond words. A trap had been set that left me ashamed and humiliated. Because of my stupidity, a terrible price was paid. Never, in a million years, had I expected this. I was convinced that he would use that picture against me. No matter what it took, there must be a way to get it back.

I became so worried which resulted in a restless night. Every time I called Donna via phone, she claimed she didn't know his whereabouts. The next day was no different.

He left me no other choice but to go out and search for him. The unsuccessful hunt led me to make another trip to visit Donna. Maybe, just possibly, he told her to lie about being there. Donna opened the door and invited me in. He really wasn't there.

The picture would not be my topic of discussion. By now, I'm sure she already knew. I stormed out of her house without saying goodbye.

Stress took a toll on me and I reported off from work. Four days later, Bill showed up at my door. He walked in as if nothing ever happened.

"Bill, what you did was a dirty rotten shame!"

With a smirk on his face, he said, "I know." Then he sat down, put his feet on the coffee table, grabbed the remote, and cut the television on.

I just stood there with my mouth wide open not wanting to believe his reactions. My grandmother would have washed my mouth out with soap had she heard the vulgar language that surfaced from my mouth directed at Bill. If I thought I was capable of beating him up, without a doubt, "it would have been on."

Instead of going back and forth with unkind words, Bill turned the television up full blast. I was steaming. You could have literally fried an egg on the top of my head. That's how hot and frustrated I became. Realizing all the yelling wasn't doing me any good made me think about lowering my voice down a notch.

"Bill, what did you do with the pictures?"

"Don't worry bout it; it's in a safe place," said sarcastic Bill.

"I would like to have it, please. What you did was an invasion of my privacy." It took a lot of energy for me to try to remain calm. That grin was still on his face.

"Too bad, so sad. I'm plannin' on showin' it to big head Jerry and yo people. Then I'm gonna mail it to your church. Your mom and dad will then see what a sweet little daughter they raised." Bill chuckled.

"Please don't do this to me. I'm begging you. I don't want to hurt my parents. They don't need to know. I'll do anything!"

"Why ain't you thought about that when you snuck off wit your boy?"

I confessed, "I'm so sorry. It will never happen again."

"Too late!" Bill said.

Desperation was beyond words. "Bill, I don't know what else to say. You know I love you."

"Do you love me enough to drop those charges?" Bill asked. "You know my other hearing is in a few days."

"I won't show up." This was blackmail, but there wasn't much to do about it. Having that picture was crucial and more important.

Bill said, "We will see."

When the day of the hearing came, I was unavailable. The court costs came in the mail. After that, I went directly to Bill for the pictures. He refused to give them to me and called me a fool. I was devastated.

Facing the other music meant having to explain to Jerry the reason for me not showing up at the hearing. He would have to know about the pictures before Bill confronted him. I asked him to meet me in front of my brother's house.

While sitting in his vehicle, the possibility was there of me losing my best friend. He tried so hard to help.

"Jerry, you know, we've been friends for a very long time, and I truly value our friendship." Jerry got ready to interrupt. "Please let me finish."

I looked him in his eyes and said, "I'm not the woman you think I am. I've done many things that I'm ashamed of. I've lied to you, much less lied to myself. Your friendship has meant more to me than you'll ever know. I was so worried that you would walk away if I told you the truth. You never judged me or looked down on me like many people and I appreciate and respect that in you. And now, I have to tell you something that I should've told you a long time ago. I don't want you to, but if you walk away, I'll understand. I don't know any easy way to tell you this except to tell it like it is."

I continued and admitted my wrong doings. "I've been doing drugs. I was clean for a while, but just the other day, I relapsed. I was over Donnas' house, and Bill was there. One thing led to another, and the next thing I knew we were all getting high. Not long after that, Bill took advantage of the situation and shot drugs in my arm. I was so spaced out, that he took a picture of me with a needle in my arm. He's planning to show it to you and my parents. Then he's going to send it to the church. I tried numerous times to get it back. He used the picture to blackmail me, so I wouldn't show up at the hearing. I don't know what else to say except that I am so sorry."

Jerry shook his head with disappointment. He didn't say much except, "Thank you for being honest with me." Then he opened the car door for me to get out. Jerry drove off, and I went home "feeling like two cents."

I disappointed my best friend as well as myself. Jerry didn't deal with women who used drugs. After that, seeing him was a rare thing and when I did, the conversation was very short. I hoped that Jerry just needed some time. Maybe someday he could find it in his heart to forgive me.

CHAPTER NINETEEN

I STAYED AWAY FROM MY PARENTS' house for a while. Bill continued to use the picture against me. Just in case I didn't want to believe it still existed, he made it his business to show it to me several times. For the moment, he had me just where he wanted.

Bill spent nights at my house anytime he wanted. He constantly popped in and out doing whatever he chose to do. I had to do whatever he asked of me. It seemed like a joke to him. I was disgusted and felt like trash. Because of my predicament, socializing with any man was out of the question.

Messing up with Jerry was a huge mistake. He was a friend beyond a friend, and I missed him. It was my fault for not being honest with him from the beginning.

Bill was a "jerk". He tried his best to be nice, but it now meant absolutely nothing to me.

Bill said, "It's been a while since I took y'all to 'Bigmomma's Place.' I gambled last night and won some doe. Dinner on me!"

Politely I said, "No thanks." Bill looked at me puzzled. He knew this was one of my favorite restaurants.

"Well, you wanna go for a ride and go to the park?" He looked at Tina and said, "Wouldn't you like that?"

Tina looked at me waiting for my response. "Thanks, but no thanks."

Bill got an attitude and used profanity in front of Alisha and Tina. "What's your problem? I'm tryin' to be nice. You say we ain't

155

doin' enough as a family. When I ask you, you actin' like you got a big chip on your shoulder."

I was silent, and Tina came and put her arms around me. Alisha started whining.

As Bill walked out the door, he said, "I'm goin' out of town for a few days. When I come back, don't look for me, or say nothin' to me. We're done. So, you can have Jerry, Sherman, or whomever you want. Just stay out my face!" Then, Bill slammed the door.

I was glad that he exited the premises. Now, I could relax and get a little peace for the moment. Comforting the kids as we sat on the couch took a lot out of me. There was no better time like the present for me to have a "heart-to-heart" talk with them.

I said, "I need you to listen really well. When your daddy talks to me like that, he doesn't mean it. He's just having some problems right now, which makes him treat me bad sometimes. Your daddy needs help."

Tina said, "Well, when he goin' get help?"

"I don't know. Real soon, I hope."

Tina said, "When I'm in bed, sometimes I hear him say bad things to you, and sometimes I hear you cry."

There were numerous times that I closed Tina's bedroom door hoping that she didn't hear Bill's vulgar language. Apparently, she heard more than I thought.

"I am so sorry you had to hear all of that, but it's going to be all right. He will get help, I promise. In the meantime, be nice to him, and don't talk back. He's a good person. He just has bad ways."

Alisha said, "Daddy's bad. Bad daddy. Bad daddy."

I was surprised to hear Alisha say that. "No, no, no, don't say that. Daddy's not bad."

I didn't want her to dislike or be afraid of him. He would never hurt or mistreat the children. The only time there was a problem concerning the kids, was when he threw Alisha on the water couch and let her scream.

Tina frowned. "I don't like Bill no more. He's mean to you." That was the very first time she had ever said that.

Alisha repeated, "He mean. No like him."

I said, "Stop saying that. He's going to get help, and then he'll be nice to mommy."

That was enough said for the moment. "Who wants to help mommy bake some cookies?"

The kids got excited and said, "Me, me."

We went into the kitchen. "Tina, hand me the sugar, flour, and the eggs. And get four sticks of butter out of the refrigerator. Give it to Alisha to give to me."

Tina found everything and said, "Here it is. What else?"

"I need the vanilla flavor. It's in a bottle on the bottom shelf."

I pulled the baking pans out of the cupboards. We made homemade delicious chocolate chip cookies--the melt-in-your-mouth kind.

Tina said, "These are so good."

Alisha said, "I like dis kind. Can I have more?"

"One more for you, and two more for Tina and that's it. You can have some more tomorrow."

Cleaning up the kitchen did not take very long. Tina rinsed all the silverware and the bowls prior to my washing dishes. After putting them in bed, I was able to relax and decide what to do the following day. Visiting my parents would not be a bad idea except for the possibility of them "chewing me out" for staying away too long. I'm glad they didn't know about the picture. It would have definitely been an issue.

CHAPTER TWENTY

THE NEXT DAY, A STORM CAME our way, so I waited until it subsided. The kids were already dressed. We headed out the door to go for a visit to my parents' house. I rang the doorbell. Mom let us in.

"Hi Mom, hi Dad." Alisha and Tina spoke as well. Dad was reading the newspaper. "Where's Lorraine?"

Mom said, "She got a job at the A&R grocery store. Today was her first day. She tried to call you and tell you the good news but couldn't reach you."

"What position did she get hired for?"

"I believe it was a cashier's position," Mom said.

"I'm glad for her."

Dad sat there continuously reading the newspaper and never looked up until twenty minutes later. "Are you all right? Do you need anything?" I didn't want to know what he sensed or if he knew anything.

"No, we're fine."

I quickly changed the subject. Dad worked in the same mill as I did, but in a different department. He had put in thirty years of service and been retired for two years. His desire was to devote his time to the ministry.

I said, "Did you hear about the plant layoff coming up in the mill? I'm probably on that list."

"Yea, I was just reading about that. It was on the news too. I heard that the lay-off would possibly affect those that have seven to nine years of service."

"Well, that would certainly include me."

"Don't worry. If that happens, God will bless you to find another job."

"I'm not worried. I hope I'm laid off. I heard they would be offering us a severance pay. In addition, I will probably be able to collect unemployment checks. That should hold me for a while."

I'm surprised you lasted this long," replied dad.

"Yeah, it has been seven long hard years. The mill is no place for me to make a lifetime career. If they offer me a severance pay, I would not hesitate to take it."

Dad and I talked about a few other things while mom was in the dining room on her sewing machine. She loved to make clothes from time to time. I'll never forget the time she made my prom dress. They couldn't afford to buy me one. The beautiful blue satin long gown with the matching jacket took her three days to make.

I had a date with a guy named Donald. He wore a black tuxedo with a powder blue silky shirt that matched my gown.

Mom also liked doing puzzles. She was good at putting the pieces together. She would leave it on the dining room table and work on it for days until it was finally completed.

"Mom, have you been doing any puzzles lately?"

"I just completed one called, "The Tower of Babylon." It had one thousand pieces to it. I had to put it away so that I could use the dining room table to work on this pattern."

"Ah, I wished I could have seen it when it was finished."

"Well, if you came here a little more often, you would have. I started it and finished it about three different times."

There was nothing for me to say after that comment. Feeding into that would have given her a reason to start on my case. I breathed a sigh of relief.

A week later, a notice from the mill came informing me of the layoff. The following Monday, I went to the unemployment office to file for benefits. After the final approval, my first check came in about two weeks. Months later, I received my severance pay. The amount was $3,250.00.

Bill was not going to find out about this. I was grateful for the money because it gave me an opportunity to catch up on some bills and to go grocery shopping. After buying Tina and Alisha some clothes, I headed straight to the bank.

While Bill was out of town, I opened up a bank account. Everything seemed to be falling into place.

Maybe Bill would decide to stay in New York, and I wouldn't have to worry about that picture anymore. My thoughts were also about giving Jerry a call, hoping he had forgiven me.

While putting away the groceries, someone unexpectedly knocked on the door. It was a couple of Bill's female friends. These were the nice and respectful ones. I assumed they were looking for Bill and invited them in.

"Hi, come on in, but if you're looking for Bill, he's not here. I think he's still out of town. I haven't seen him for about four or five days."

"We didn't come to see Bill. We came to see how you are doing, and if there is anything that we can do. Isn't that awful what happened?"

I stood there with a puzzled look on my face, not knowing what they meant. They immediately realized I was clueless.

"Sarah, I'm sorry. I guess you didn't hear about Jerry."

"What about him?"

"Someone shot him. He's dead!"

I took two steps backward and almost fainted. "No, no, this can't be happening, not Jerry!" I began to cry, and they tried to console me.

It was true. At first, I thought maybe Bill did it until reading the article in the newspaper concerning what really happened.

I couldn't sleep that night after hearing the bad news. While sitting in the living room chair, I wondered why bad things happen to good people. He was a good man. Furthermore, he never bothered anyone unless he had a good reason. He helped so many people. I just didn't understand. Jerry was my best friend and now he's gone.

Lorraine came over my house to stay for a few days to be there with me. She only left out when she had to go to work.

A couple of days after Jerry died, Bill showed up. I was upstairs lying in bed and my sister opened the door. Bill pushed his way through the door. He didn't see me downstairs, so he made his way upstairs. I was lying across the bed still saddened about the news.

Bill took one look at me and said, "Sorry to hear bout your lover man, Jerry."

All of a sudden, I snapped and stood up screaming, "Get out! Get out!"

Lorraine ran upstairs to make sure Bill didn't put his hands on me.

Bill said, "Glad he's dead. He got his justice. What goes round comes round. If somebody hadn't beaten me to the punch, I would have done it myself."

I couldn't take it anymore and picked up the baseball bat that was behind the door. Bill saw the look in my eyes and ran down the steps almost knocking Lorraine down as he flew out the door. I yelled down the steps.

"I hate you, Bill, I hate you!"

The private funeral was only for the family, but somehow I managed to get in. This would be the last time for me to see Jerry. During the processional, fighting back the tears was impossible. I had lost my best friend for good. His family managed to hold up.

Bill seemed pleased he didn't have to worry about Jerry anymore. My heart was heavy and I wanted Bill out of my life more than ever. He could shove that picture...!

Bill seized every opportunity he could to be with the kids. Every time Alisha got mad at me, she would want her daddy. Other times, she didn't like her daddy anymore. Deep down inside, I think she was crazy about him. As she got older, whenever she saw him, her eyes would light up as long as we weren't arguing. I must say that Bill spoiled her. He gave her just about anything she wanted. He would give her money, candy, and buy her toys.

When it came to me, Bill was "plain ole" stingy. He was freehearted with everyone else. He would give his last dollar up if someone needed it--especially his grandmother. She was "his heart."

Bill's grandmother died a few months later. She lived in the country and was very precious and full of wisdom. Every now and then, Bill and I would drive up to see her. That's when I realized how close they were. If she asked Bill to do something, and he could not, he would go out of his way making sure she got the help she needed. She helped raise him, and Bill always spoke very highly of her. When she died, I put my feelings aside and went to pay my respects. Bill wept.

After returning from the funeral, Bill started slowly bringing clothes back into my house. Every time I would pack them up, he would find an excuse not to take them.

"Bill, you need to take your bag of clothes out of here."

"Oh, I'll get them later." Later would never come.

Bill didn't threaten me about the picture as much anymore. I guess he assumed he had me where he wanted me and didn't need to. To this day, I still don't know what happened to that picture.

"You're not moving back in here, so you might as well take your clothes."

It did not matter what I said or did, getting rid of him was next to impossible. He was like a "thorn in my side," and I needed a solution to resolve things permanently. After weighing things out, my decision was to move to another city without Bill finding out.

CHAPTER TEWNTY-ONE

MY PLANS WERE TO WAIT FOR Bill to leave town again, and then move. In the meantime, searching for rental property became a priority in my life. The money in the bank left over from my severance pay came in handy. There was enough to cover the rent, security deposit and to pay a moving company. Paying people from the street would have been cheaper, but there would have been a risk of Bill finding out where I lived.

Searching through the newspaper was my best option. There were quite a few houses available in Springfield, Colorado. This was 45 minutes away, which was close enough to my family, yet far enough to keep from running into Bill.

Phone calls were made to about seven or eight listings. Only three people returned my calls. One man said he had just rented out the house. Another person said there would be a fee of $25 to do a credit check. I wasn't interested. My credit needed repaired. The last person that returned my call stated she would be showing the house on Saturday from one to 3 p.m. I gave my name and number and made an appointment.

When Saturday came, I anxiously went to see the house. It took me a while to find it because it was on a dead end street. After taking one look, a quick decision resulted. This was not for me, but I would at least check the inside out. An abandoned house stood to the right of the premises. To the left was an old-castle looking house. Looking at it gave me the creeps.

As I went up the walkway, someone was just leaving. Mrs.

Swooney was the property owner and showed the house. The fully carpeted living and dining room was nice. The rooms were freshly painted. The small kitchen did not have a lot of cabinet space, which was a necessity. There were three bedrooms upstairs. The worst part of the house was that the bathroom and laundry room happened to be in the unfinished gloomy basement.

"Thank you, Mrs. Swooney, for showing me the house. I will let you know if I'm still interested no later than tomorrow."

"If you are interested, you have to put something down to hold it."

"Okay," I replied. The area as well as the bathroom in the spooky-looking basement affected my decision. I had no intention on calling her back.

Buying a newspaper had become a daily part of my routine. Some of the houses in the paper sounded promising except for the price of the rent. Something affordable was what I needed.

Searching for the right place took a lot of time. One place caught my attention. The house was in Marion, at 1801 Vineyard St., about thirty minutes away from Denver. I called the phone number listed in the paper and made an appointment for 6 p.m. the next day. Finding the house wasn't hard. Mr. Philip would be the person for me to meet. He was pulling up upon my arrival.

"Hello, are you Mr. Philip?"

"Yes, I am, are you Sarah Jones?"

"Yes." We shook hands and went into the house. Mr. Philip was a short and stout built man. I assumed he was in his late 50's. He was very polite and very thorough in showing and telling me about the house.

When I first walked in, there was a hallway entrance. On the first floor, to my left, was a spacious living room with light-brown carpet. The fireplace was beautiful even though it wasn't real. Hanging on the ceiling was a striking fan with a gold-antique light fixture.

Mr. Philip said, "The house has been checked for termites and recently winterized. The house is in pretty good shape."

"That's good."

Mr. Philip took me into the dining room. There was no carpet in there, but the wooden floors were nicely polished. It was roomy enough for me.

The eat-in kitchen area had plenty of cupboard space. The appliances were already in place for the next tenant. The location of the powder room was on the right corner of the kitchen. The lavender wallpaper made it look "fit for a king." The unfinished basement had hook-ups for a washer and a dryer and was not spooky.

On the second floor were three bedrooms, two large, and one small. The master bedroom had a walk-in closet. To the right was a spacious bathroom with a shower. All of the rooms were exceptionally clean.

Mr. Philip asked, "Well, what do you think?"

"I like it!"

Mr. Philip went on to explain. "I originally promised this house to someone else, but they're a little slow producing the money. If they don't have it by next week, I'll contact you and you can have the house. Just make sure you have the security deposit, and as soon as you pay the first month's rent, I'll give you the key."

"Ok, thank you!" I was grateful and left feeling reassured that the house was mine. Now, I could finally get some peace from Bill.

Mr. Philip would have to give me his official word before I packed anything. A week later, the call came.

"The house is yours, if you're still interested."

This phone call made my day. "Yes, I'm still interested. Thank you. I have the security deposit and first month's rent. When can we meet?"

Mr. Phillips said, "I have a business meeting near your town on Wednesday, so how about we meet at the house after that. Let's say, about 2 p.m."

"I'll be there!" I hung the phone up and leaped for joy. Tina was in school and Alisha looked at me wondering what happened. I couldn't wait to tell my parents the good news. Alisha went upstairs to play while I called mom.

"Hello mom, guess what?"

Mom said, "You sound awfully excited. What's going on?"

Overflowing with bliss, I blurted, "I'm moving! I found me another house!"

Mom asked, "Where at?"

"It's in Marion, on Vineyard Street. I am so excited."

"I didn't know you were looking for another place to live. Are you getting evicted?"

"No mom. There was just too many things that needed fixed and the landlord wasn't taking care of it fast enough." I dared not tell mom the real reason.

"Well, if you're happy, I'm happy for you."

"I'm very happy. Mom, can I bring some boxes to store in your garage? I promise they won't be in your way."

"Sometimes your dad parks his car in the garage, so as long as you don't block the entrance that should be fine."

"Thanks mom, I'll talk to you later."

For the rest of the week, I went to different grocery stores and stocked up on boxes. An opportunity to pack would come soon.

I met Mr. Philip on Wednesday and gave him the rent and security deposit. After signing the lease, he gave me the keys. The new set of keys in my hand and the lease quickly became a symbol of freedom. This would be the beginning of a brand-new fresh start. Exhilaration and novelty, as well as relief, filled me.

Bill kept coming around but hadn't said anything for a while about going out of town. Asking him would have aroused suspicion.

Three weeks later, Bill claimed he was leaving. That day couldn't come fast enough. The second month's rent would soon be due. Moving before Bill left was unthinkable.

Bill said, "Carl and I are goin' to New York this weekend. Got business to take care of, you hear?"

"Okay, just be careful." I had to play it very cool. If I didn't, Bill might change his mind and not go.

Bill added, "Be back soon as I can."

Once he leaves, the moving process would begin. The fact of not knowing how much time it would take to get everything out the house made me feel a little nervous. In addition, Bill was not specific about the length of time he would be gone. I dared not ask him. Eventually, he would mention it.

Finally, two weeks and one day later, Bill said, "Need you to whip up lunch for the road. We're out of here round 11 p.m." This was on a Thursday night.

"What would you like?" I asked.

Bill stated, "A couple of sandwiches. Kielbasa is cool if we got it. Oh, yeah, and somethin' to snack on."

"Okay. I'll start fixing it around 10," I calmly said.

Maybe Bill thought I was being too cool about everything. He started to pace and warned, "Hope you not plannin' on cheatin' on me. I will hurt somebody up in here."

Rolling my eyes, I said, "Oh, please, that's the furthest thing on my mind."

Bill left to go down the street for a while so I ran down to my brother's house. After announcing the good news, I asked to use the phone. There was not much time to find an available moving company in the yellow pages.

Almost everyone seemed to be booked up for this particular weekend. Pressure weighed heavily on me. Finally, "Henson's Moving Company" received one cancellation. I was relieved. They gave me a price of $200.00 and would be available on Saturday at 7 a.m. After making payment over the phone and giving them the necessary information, I returned to the house to prepare lunch for the traveling men.

Bill and Carl were supposed to leave at 11p.m., on Thursday night. By the time they left, it was about 2 a.m. In light of my being fatigue and the lateness of the hour, it stopped me from getting anything accomplished that night.

I had to get a little rest. The clock was set for 6:30 a.m. I awakened Tina and Alisha, fed them, and took them to the babysitter's house. Telling them about the move would come later that day.

I picked up the boxes from my dad's garage and returned home to start packing. Starting in the kitchen seemed to be the most sensible thing to do. The newspapers saved enabled me to pack up all my dishes. The books as well as the miscellaneous items in the living and dining room were next. Now, the van could be loaded. Because of mechanical problems, Bill didn't want to chance taking the vehicle on his road trip. He arranged for another ride.

A couple of neighbors peeked out the window while watching me carry out boxes. No one offered to help. The almost loaded van caused me to be completely exhausted. The task was too immense to finish by myself.

I did not want to bother my family. However, Lorraine was most eager to lend a hand. She came down, hopped into my vehicle, and got busy. We were both glad she didn't have to work that day. My dad called a couple of people from the church to come help. My brother did his usual complaining but helped tremendously. They wondered why I hadn't asked them in the first place.

"I didn't want to bother you--especially at the last minute, but I sure do appreciate you."

It took about five to six hours before finishing, including taking a break to eat and rest. Because of the help, I was able to take just about everything that would fit in the van, including the TV's and stereo equipment. This took several trips.

Gratitude overwhelmed me, and I paid a little cash to everyone that helped. I explained to them that my location for the time being needed to remain a secret.

While it was still daylight, I took Alisha and Tina for a walk and explained to them about the move.

Tina asked, "Why are we movin'?"

"Because we need a new house," I said.

Alisha wanted to know if her daddy was coming.

I explained, "No, and he can't come and visit us anymore because he didn't get the help that he needed. But guess what?"

They both said, "What?"

I reassured them that this was a positive thing. "We got a very nice house, and there are a lot of kids that live on that street. So that means you will be having new friends to play with."

Tina whined, "But what about my friends here?"

Leaning on her with a smile and a fingertip tap to her nose, I said, "We can come and get them sometimes. In fact, after we get situated, you can have a sleepover and invite all your friends. How about that?"

Tina smiled with her wide grin. Alisha clapped her hands in agreement. After breaking the news to them, we went back inside my brother's house. We would be staying there for the night.

I needed a little time to myself. Therefore, I drove to a nearby park, sat on the bench, and contemplated about the new upcoming changes in my life.

Finally realizing that the relationship was truly over broke my heart. That picture wasn't as important any more. It happened. If Bill wanted to show someone, I couldn't stop him. Many regrets were obvious. I needed total freedom and my sanity back now--not tomorrow. My life was passing by before my very own eyes. In spite of my youth, I was beginning to age. The cycle of abuse had to stop.

The next day seemed to arrive in no time. The movers met me at the old house. Since there was a stove at the new house, the old one stayed. Everything else would need moved. The company workers had everything packed and brought to the new resident in less than four hours.

I gave instructions to the movers of where to place the furniture. One of them was nice enough to put our beds together, although it wasn't in the contract. I was very grateful.

While the kids watched tapes, I thoroughly cleaned both bathrooms. Then a lot of time was spent wiping down the cupboards in the kitchen and putting away the dishes, pots, and pans. I was tired and the kids were hungry.

Three frozen dinners went in the oven. Cooking a full course meal "was not happening."

The next day I finished cleaning the closets and put all the clothes away. After that, I went to the old house to sweep and mop. My intentions were to leave it in satisfactory condition.

My mom always said, "Do unto others as you would have others do unto you."

On Monday, Tina transferred to her new school. Because of her shyness, it took her a while to adjust and make new friends. She deeply missed her old playmates. I had to think of fun things to do to keep her from being so sad. Alisha seemed to be okay.

I used the pay phone on the corner street to call the phone company. They gave me a new private number, which would be on that Friday. Therefore, I would be without a phone for a whole week, which seemed like eternity. The cable company didn't have any available slots until that following Saturday.

The gas, lights, and water were already on. I just needed it disconnected from the old house and all utilities changed over in my name at the new house. Everything was coming together as planned.

When Bill finally came back, he realized the house was vacant. He started his search for me by stopping by my brother's and then my parents' house. None of my family members would give him any information.

Lorraine and Mark said, "He was furious."

Bill told them, "Don't matter at all. She ain't far, and if she was, no states in America goin' keep me from findin' her. We belong together. She's mine!"

CHAPTER TWENTY-TWO

HERE I AM IN MY NEW HOUSE. The peace seemed to have vanished. At night, sleep was next to impossible--especially when I heard a noise in the settling house. After a while, the sounds had gotten so immense that it seemed to be my haven by day and a haunted castle by night. Worrying about what Bill might do if he found me was at its peak.

Lorraine would come and spend the night sometimes, and I would be glad. Resting at night became easier when she was there while hoping she would move in.

Lorraine began dating someone from the area and expressed the fact of wanting her own place. "Sarah, let me know if you hear of any apartments for rent in this area."

"I'll check the paper and keep my eyes and ears opened," I promised. I was relieved that she considered moving in this area. The search began.

Several weeks later, Lorraine said, "My friend, Darvin, said that his uncle has an apartment building around the corner from you. I made an appointment to see it tomorrow."

"Wonderful!" I exclaimed, hoping for the best. A family member close to me would be great since there weren't many people in the area that I knew. In the meantime, Lorraine stayed all night so it would be convenient for her to make it to her appointment.

Lorraine said, "I'm going out tonight. They have a D.J. at "Harry's Bar." I probably won't get in until late, so don't wait up for me."

"Okay, when you knock on the door, just call my name, so I'll know it's you."

Her going out didn't bother me since I would only be alone a partial of the night. Even though the children were there, another adult in the house just made me more at ease.

I waited up for Lorraine even though she told me not to. She came in around 2 a.m. The rest of the night was peaceful.

The next day, Lorraine went to see the apartment. The potential new home for her was within walking distance from my house. She came back with a Tina-like grin, which meant great news.

Lorraine exclaimed, "I got the apartment!"

With a sigh of relief, I said, "Yes!" I was so overjoyed because if I needed her, she would be just a couple blocks away.

"Do you like the apartment? What does it look like?" These kinds of questions came out of my mouth like "rapid fire." I was probably more excited for her than she was.

Lorraine said, "There are three floors in the building. The only available one was the attic apartment. It will do for now."

She didn't go into much detail about what the apartment looked like on the inside and moved in a week later. I gave her some pots, pans, dishes, sheets, and other miscellaneous items. Settling in didn't take her long.

Even though Lorraine now had her own place, she continued to stop by and visit off and on. Every now and then, she stayed all night.

So far, Bill hadn't found me yet. However, it was hard not to worry. Come nightfall, I felt like a bomb ready to explode. Being fearless wasn't easy when heading to bed with no other adult in the house.

My overly tired self slept for a couple of hours one night until hearing a knock on my door, which jolted me out of my slumber. Jumping up, I looked at the clock. A sigh of relief came since the clock displayed 2 a.m. No doubt, it was Lorraine. I got up, headed downstairs, and opened the curtain in the window of the door.

My sleepy eyes suddenly got big--very—big. It was not Lorraine, but Bill. I closed the curtain quickly, hoping he would go away, and practically froze in my steps.

He knew that I saw him, so he knocked again--this time louder. I didn't want him to awake the kids and was fearful of opening the door. My heart pounded.

I quietly said, "What do you want?"

Bill said, "My mom died, had a heart attack. Please let me in. I need to talk to you bout takin' Alisha wit me to the funeral."

Despite his quiet, serious demeanor, I began to panic and sensed danger. Fear was at its peak. While pacing back and forth, my heart rate was rising. Instantly, I remembered the dream and refused to open that door--no matter what.

My knuckles clenched the curtain, which soaked up some of the sweat of my palm. I twisted the drapery--pulling it back open just a little. My voice started to crack while verbally responding.

The only logical thing for me to say was, "Well, I'm sorry to hear about your mother. You have my condolence. I was in bed and it's very late. I'll try to get in touch with you tomorrow and we can talk about the arrangements."

I didn't know if he was lying or not, and hoped he wouldn't "stoop so low" as to lie about something like that just to get in. Regardless, I was not opening the door. Even if his mother really had died, Alicia would not be going with him to the funeral. He might have decided to keep her there just to hurt me.

In New York, it would have been very hard for me to find her, because he knew so many people. I will not take that chance nor risk my life by going with him. He always told me; whenever he was angry, that he couldn't wait for an opportunity to get me back up there.

My clammy hands closed the curtain again while he stood on the other side of the door. My heart pounded even more as if a heart attack was surfacing. I couldn't figure out how he found me.

Immediately, Bill kicked the door once, then twice--as hard as he could. The locks broke off and the door flew open. Flinching, I panicked while moving backwards.

I tried to run, but he snatched me. He grabbed the hose to the vacuum sweeper and started hitting me across my face. Pistol-whipping me came next, which generated blood dripping from my head. He punched me in the chest. When I screamed, he pointed the gun at me and told me to shut up. Then he grabbed me by my hair, pulled me upstairs to my bedroom, and closed the door. The kids awakened from hearing the commotion.

While still in bed, Tina yelled, "Mommy, what's wrong?"

Bill lied and said, "Yo Mammy is ok. She's crying cause my mother died. Go back to sleep. She will be all right."

He pointed the gun at me and made me reassure them that everything was okay. Once I did, they drifted back to sleep unaware of the nature of Bill's madness.

Bill glared at me and said. "By the way, tell yo stupid sister to cover her tracks next time. I followed her after she left the bar the other night. She led me straight to you and still ain't realized it, so you need to thank her. Did you think you could hide from me forever? You could've gone to Alaska. I still would've tracked you down."

Bill continued. My quiet cries meant nothing as I begged for mercy. He wouldn't listen, and broke the legs of a wooden chair in the room and started hitting me across my knees. An indescribable pain shot through me. He grabbed my hair again and swung me around the room. Every time I fell into something, his clutch led to a continuation of the abuse. He threatened to shoot me on the spot if I screamed one more time.

"This is the last night of your life, hoe. Got four bullets in this gun. One for each kid, one for you, and the last one for me. My mother's dead, and I ain't got nothin' else, to live for, but first, I'm goin' to get the likin' of seein' you suffer a slow death. I hate you. You caused my wife and my mom to die. You broke my mom's heart when you put me out. She ain't been the same since. Now you gonna pay for my pain and sufferin'. Murderer! Murderer! Murderer!"

There was no logic to what he said and no time to dispute things. My main concern was saving my children's life and mine. There was unbearable pain all over my body and blood dripped everywhere. I started saying anything and everything I thought he wanted to hear.

"I'm sorry, Bill If you want to, you can move back into the house with me! We really need to try to work things out! I'm willing to marry, honor, and obey you if you will still have me! I love you, Bill! Please don't do this! Think about the children! They love you!

They have their whole life ahead of them! Please don't take it away! Take mine if you have to, but please don't hurt the children! They're innocent!"

No matter what I said, Bill wasn't buying it. "You lying, you lying! And it ain't goin' do you no good! You good as dead…!"

I got on my bruised, aching knees and pleaded with Bill again. "Please, Bill, please don't hurt us!"

"Shut up!" Bill demanded. "You should have thought bout that a long time ago. You think I'm stupid, don't you?"

Before I could respond, Bill punched me in the mouth. Seconds later, my lip swelled up, and blood flowed freely from my mouth. I tried to reach for a tissue. He hit me again.

I started silently praying that Lorraine would knock on the door. This was a matter of life or death. I needed her. Where was she?

Bill seemed to read my mind. "Where's yo family now? The police ain't even comin'. I could easily get away wit killing you!"

I got ready to plead again, and he yelled, "Shut up! I ain't goin' tell you no more! You know what? You ain't even worth it." After saying all of that, he proceeded to play mind games.

"If you wanna live, you goin' to have to kill me first. Let's see where your heart is." He held the gun out in my direction and said, "Take this gun and shoot me!"

I trembled hysterically.

"You heard me! Take this gun and shoot me. If you don't, if you think I kicked yo … now, you can't imagine what I'm goin' do to you next. Now do as I said or get ready for round two. Cause when I get finished wit you, you goin' wish you had!"

Bill put the gun in my wobbly hands, took the safety off, and pointed it toward his head. "Now shoot me, you…!"

My state of mind had me literally feeling that I was leaving my body. A quiet voice within said, "Hang in there. I will bring you out. This is not the end."

Reality set back in. Blood mixed with sweat poured from my face. The thought crossed my mind that he was only trying to trick me to see if I would pull the trigger. Then he would laugh and say there were no bullets in the gun and beat me worse for attempting to pull the trigger. This was a difficult situation. My head was pounding worse than ever. My thoughts became as fragments within a still-blowing storm. Bill made one more attempt to get me to pull the trigger. I knew that time was running out.

Thinking back over my life and the mess I made was obvious. My parents tried to steer me in the right direction, but I wouldn't listen. My thoughts were that I could handle whatever came my way. All I ever wanted was a return of the same love that I had given.

Every time Bill abused me, I ignored the warning signals. My belief was so strong about Bill changing that I allowed myself to fall into a series of traps.

I didn't want to die. My desire was to live and raise my children to the best of my ability. I've wasted so much time trying to please a man that never meant me any good from the start. The time and love should have gone towards my family and a successful life. I squandered on this villain.

The girls deserved an apology as well as an assurance of my love for them. I needed to ask them to forgive me. My parents, needed to hear that I loved them, as well, and was sorry for being a disobedient child. I felt doomed and desperately longed for a second chance to make things right.

Bill opened the gun and showed me the bullets. The beatings started escalating. I was helpless but noticed the cracked window. The thought briefly crossed my mind to jump out the window, but was too worried about the children. My fear about that escape attempt was that he would shoot me in the back.

Strength began leaving my body as I became less and less competent at thwarting the blows. Exhausted, I blocked weakly--then not at all.

God was the only One to whom I could turn to. Silently, I started praying while crying my heart out as I slid down the bloody wall of my bedroom. "God, help me! Don't let him hurt us. If I must go, protect and save my children. They need you. Please, Lord, Please!"

I thought my prayers were silent. However, Bill heard me.

"Shut up, shut up, God ain't hearin' your little stupid…, and he ain't goin' help you!"

Then, Bill took the gun and pointed it at me.

My prayers and cries got louder and louder, "Please God, I'm sorry for everything, so very sorry. Forgive me for all my sins! Please, please come to my rescue!"

Bill started laughing. The louder I prayed, the louder Bill laughed. He put his finger on the trigger. Closing my eyes, I covered my face. The end seemed imminent. Judgment day had come for me.

Just then, we both heard a movement in the children's room. Someone or something was walking around. Bill walked away and opened the door to the kid's room. They were snoring at such a decibel level that I could hear it from my room. The girls were sound asleep. I think it was an angel giving me a way to escape.

Bill continued to search the kid's room with the gun in his hand. There was so much pain in my body but no time to think about it. A little strength came back from a power source not fully explainable. Quickly but quietly getting up off the floor, I took off running with all my might down fifteen or more steps. My blood left a trail. Bill chased me, unsuccessfully, and could have easily shot me in the back. My guardian angel, once again had my back.

When I got outside, the brisk-night air sliced my screams. At "bullet speed," I ran to my next-door neighbor's house and banged on the door as hard as I could. They opened the door just in time, and Bill took off running in a different direction. He had tormented me about two and a half hours.

The neighbors looked at me in "awe." They handed me the phone without asking any questions. My appearance told everything. I called the police, and they were on their way.

All kind of thoughts were going through my mind. *How could I have left my children there all alone? What kind of mother would do such a thing?* While I was waiting impatiently, I paced the floor while crying and praying. *God, please keep my children safe. Don't let him go back in my house.* I would have never forgiven myself if something had happened to my children.

Sirens came from all directions. The police were there in no time. Panicking, I stammered, "Officer, please check the house! My children are in there and he got a gun!" They went into the house with their guns pointed out and checked all the rooms.

Linda Foster

While I waited outside, the other officers asked me several questions. "What's his name? What does he look like? How tall is he? What was he wearing? What direction did he go?"

I answered the questions to the best of my ability. My mind was still cloudy from worrying about my children.

The police officers finally came out of the house. "He's not in there." Sighing with relief, I slumped down to the curb.

In the meantime, the police called the ambulance. I asked them if they could take the kids to their aunt's house and they did. The children did not need to see me in this shape. The officers told the girls I needed to go to the hospital and that I would explain it to them later.

The hospital examined me thoroughly. They x-rayed my head, chest, and legs. My right fractured knee swelled up tremendously. I had a concussion. My head as well as the inside and outside of my mouth needed stitches. Bruises were all over my body. The hospital treated me and kept me for a couple of days for observation. I was in a lot of pain, but yet alive and grateful.

CHAPTER TWENTY-THREE

AFTER LEAVING THE HOSPITAL, the healing process began and my bewildered children deserved an explanation. My face literally looked deformed as if a Mack truck ran over me. They wondered what happened to me and why was I limping. I told them Bill hurt me because I wouldn't open the door to let him in, and now we have to stay away from him for good. He needed help so he wouldn't do those bad things anymore.

When my dad heard about what transpired, he was enraged. He almost laid his religion down to take matters into his own hands. My mother was very upset but had to talk some sense into my father quickly before matters got any worse.

After coming home from the hospital, Lorraine cried when she saw my appearance She blamed herself and felt so bad that she didn't come back to my house that night. My brother went looking for him. It took a lot to get him mad. The police searched everywhere for Bill. Days and weeks went by, but Bill seemed to have vanished.

The doctor put me on bed rest for a few days because of the concussion and trauma to my body. Lorraine and my sister-in-law came over to help as much as they could. I knew they couldn't be there all the time. They had their own lives to live, but I appreciated what help they could give me.

After a few days of rest, I tried to do things around the house as much as possible. Staying busy helped to keep my mind occupied. However, that fear wouldn't go away. Bill was out there somewhere, and he knew where to find me. Rumor had it that he left town shortly after the incident and went back to New York. I was not so sure about that. Even if he did, I knew he would be coming back, more dangerous than ever.

My nights became more restless than ever. Frequently, I peeked out the window. Every time a car door shut, my hand was on the telephone. Sometimes, I didn't know if I was "coming or going."

I decided to go to the doctor to inform him what was going on and how I felt. He prescribed sleeping pills, but I would not take them. The thought of going to sleep would leave me feeling vulnerable.

Coffee kept me company half the night to keep from going to sleep. I was in a state of turmoil.

This stressful routine repeated itself night after night. The agony was too much for me to bear. It was time to get out of this house--and soon, but I didn't know where to go. My family's house would be the first place that Bill would look and wait patiently for me to come out. That would have been a careless decision.

I needed professional help. The search in the phone book under the "Abuse" section, led me to find a hotline number for battered women. After calling and explaining my situation, they advised me to get out of the house immediately. Quickly, I packed some clothes and miscellaneous items for us. We went to meet a designated volunteer who drove us to a shelter where I stayed in hiding for sixty days.

As they showed us around in the building, I noticed the sanctuary toward the back. The doors were always open and anyone could go there at any time. It took about an hour for the whole intake process and explanation of rules. I put the children to bed and went to the sanctuary. No one was there, so I went to the altar, got on my knees, and had a "heart to heart" talk with the Lord:

Here I am Lord. I really don't know where to start, but feel the need to be real with you because you already know all about me. I'm tired, Lord. This life I've lived, I can't do it no more. I've tried drinking. I've tried drugs, and I've been in wrong relationships. It's obvious I been looking for love in all the wrong places because nothing seems to work for me. Compromising hasn't even helped, and now, I've made a big mess of my whole life. I know it was you that protected me when I should've been dead so many times. Thank you! You were trying to tell me the whole time to walk away but I didn't listen to you. You warned me in my dreams, and I didn't take heed. Well, Lord, I'm sorry, so sorry. Please forgive me and fill this void in my life. I want to be happy again. I want that unspeakable joy I've heard about. I need you to walk and talk with me. From this day forward, please order and guide my footsteps. Amen!

After this prayer, a miraculous sense of peace came over me like never before. I felt like a brand-new person. The change in my life was inevitable, and I apologized to my children the next day.

During this transitional period, Tina went to school, and I was able to receive counseling. We had group meetings every day, and it helped me to talk openly about my problems to those who had similar experiences. They understood where I was coming from.

The one question that constantly came up was, "Why did you continue to have a relationship with a man that abused you?"

The majority of our answers were, "Because I loved him," or, "Because he threatened me if I ever left him what he would do." Many of us existed in the middle. Some of the women said they stayed because it was their only means of financial support.

We were restricted from letting anyone know our whereabouts. I notified my parents that we were in a shelter getting some help.

The kids were fine. Alisha had other children to play with. The toys kept her busy in the big playroom. Tina felt like a big sister to the smaller children, and that made her feel special. She pretended to be their schoolteacher.

The only time I came out of the shelter within those sixty days was to take care of business or see a doctor. Someone from the agency drove me to all my appointments, waited for me, and bought me back safely. My transferred mail went to a post office box. Lorraine checked on my house from time to time.

There were speakers that came to the shelter to talk about self-esteem, independent living, getting back into the workforce, and learning to say no and mean it. These were just some of the great topics discussed as well as ways to apply them to our own lives.

By the time my sixty days were up, I realized that there was hope. I can turn this bad situation around for my good. You see, Bill made me feel that I was a nobody and never would be anybody. I'm now learning that I am somebody no matter what people think or say about me. I have strengths that need brought out and weaknesses to overcome. I can't expect people to do it for me. I have to do it for myself. This is my journey. I've made the mistakes and now I must travel.

There's not enough room for you to go with me on my journey. You can steer me in the direction that you think I should go, but if my mind is not willing, it just won't work. I need to accomplish my own mission, and need to learn the lessons planned for me along the way. I can't go under it nor go around it. I have to go through it.

Timing is everything. Your time is not my time, and my time is not your time. In addition, while I'm on my travels, I have no time to look back. Could have, should have, and would have will just not do. Therefore, if I've learned from my mistakes, I am free. I can't change where I've been, but can certainly change where I'm going.

I went home feeling encouraged. When fear tried to enter my mind, I replaced it immediately with positive thoughts. "I am an over comer."

Retraining my mind helped to renew my strength. A new sense of relaxation and confidence replaced the dismay and uncertainty to which I had become so accustomed.

The first thing I did after coming home from the shelter was apologize to my parents. Then I went to church. The choir sang the song, "Oh Happy Day." Tears streamed down my face as I listened to the words. Then, the time came for the sermon. I received a rich word. The topic was "He's all I need." I went home feeling revived.

Three months had passed since I last saw or heard from Bill. One morning, while fixing breakfast, Lorraine knocked on the door. I thought she just wanted to join us for breakfast.

"Good morning, Lorraine. You're up kind of early."

Lorraine looked me straight in the eyes and didn't beat around the bush. "Sarah, you need to make a phone call to New York because I heard that Bill is dead."

"What!"

Lorraine repeated herself. "I heard he's dead! You better call and find out!"

The kids and I quickly went to Lorraine's house. After being in the shelter all that time, my telephone service was off at my request.

Donna would be the first person to call. She told me the same story, but it wasn't sinking in. My heart started pounding, and I looked for my phone book and found Jason's phone number. He lived in New York and was Bill's uncle. If anyone knew, it would be him.

"Hello! Is this Jason?"

"Yes, it is." He didn't recognize my voice, so, he said, "Who is this?"

"This is Sarah." There was silence on the phone for about ten to fifteen seconds. Just in case it wasn't true, I was skeptical about asking him such a thing.

Jason finally broke the ice and said, "I guess you heard about Bill. I'm sorry, it is true." He sounded sad.

Shaken by the confirmed news, I had to sit down as he told the story.

Jason said, "Well, as you know, Bill just had a birthday. We were all drinking and partying. Bill and his cousin Wayne talked about committing a robbery on the other side of town. I tried my best to talk them out of it because they were drunk. I knew they would get caught, but they wouldn't listen, especially Bill. When Bill went to look for his gun, it was gone. Somebody stole it. Bill was disturbed and went in the kitchen to get a butcher knife. He was determined to get his gun back. At first, he blamed Wayne for taking it, but they soon hugged and made up, but before we knew it, they were arguing again."

Jason went on to explain. "Bill took his shirt off and started swearing. He said, 'I'm tired of this…'."

Wayne picked up his own gun. Bill still had the knife in his hand while heading in his direction."

Jason paused a moment and then continued. "So Bill goes, 'Oh, you wanna shoot me? Well, go ahead, I'm ready to go.' Bill started toward his cousin with the knife in his hand. Wayne fired a warning shot into the ceiling, but Bill kept walking toward Wayne as if he was going to stab him. Wayne had no choice but to defend himself. He shot Bill dead in the chest."

There was, again, silence on the phone. I think Jason was sobbing. "After Wayne shot him, Bill stumbled back, got up, and looked at his cousin in the face. 'You done shot me. I can't believe you did dis! You killed me'!"

"Bill started wobbling to the stairway and said, 'Help me, help me!' His voice had begun to be very faint. His last words were, 'somebody take me to the hospital.' He held one hand over his chest. Then everything started coming out of him and it was all over. He was dead."

As he was telling me the story, tears ran down my face, but I did not break down. I was having mixed emotions. The reality of it all hadn't quite hit me yet.

"I am so sorry, Jason. I am truly sorry." That was all I could say.

Jason said, "Call me later and I'll let you know the funeral arrangements, but before you hang up I need to tell you something else."

"Yes?" In my mind, I wondered what more could there be.

Jason said, "I hate to be the one to tell you this, but he was planning to sneak in town the day after his birthday to finish you off and kill you."

Dumbfounded, I asked, "How do you know that?"

Jason said, "Because he told me. I tried to talk him out of that one, too. I was hoping he was just rambling on, you know, being drunk and all, but he was serious. Something tells me he would have."

All of a sudden, my stomach felt funny. I had heard enough. After getting off the phone, I left the kids with Lorraine and went home. I got down on my knees and prayed, thanking God repeatedly for his love and protection.

No matter how bad our relationship had been, I planned to take the kids and pay my respect. After the confirmed arrangements, we caught the bus to New York. Donna traveled with us. The bus took approximately seven to eight hours to get there.

Prior to that, I had to explain to Alisha that her daddy passed away. I sat her down on the couch and said, "Something has happened to your daddy, and we won't get to see him anymore." Alisha would have been turning four years old that following month.

Alisha asked, "Where's he at?"

There was no easy answer for me to give her. "He died." She must not have fully understood me because she didn't show any reaction. She would get a fuller explanation later.

Tina, on the other hand, just wanted to know if I was going to cry at the funeral. I couldn't answer her and just hugged her. She said that if I was going to cry, she didn't want to go. She said she never wanted to see me cry again. I felt it would be best to leave her with my parents.

His death did not really sink in until seeing him lying in the casket. Then, I just broke down completely. Then, Alisha started crying. She didn't quite understand what was going on, but she knew something wasn't right.

Next, she started screaming, "I want my daddy! I want my daddy!" I couldn't seem to pull myself together to comfort her.

Alisha was concerned about me, too. "Don't cry, mommy! Please don't cry!" Alisha wiped my tears with her hand, put her arms around me, and kissed me on my cheek.

Donna picked Alisha up and took her to the casket. She took a long look at her daddy. I believe she realized at this point that he was gone for good. She bent over and kissed him. When the pallbearers got ready to close the casket, Alisha waved her hand and said, "Bye, bye daddy. I love you. Bye, bye!"

After the funeral, we went straight home. While traveling, I closed my tearful eyes and thought about Bill. Our relationship was not supposed to end this way.

While taking a deep sigh of relief and sitting back in my seat, a sense of peace came over me. I knew from this point on, my life would never be the same.

Epilogue

Unfortunately, I learned the hard way, and realize now, that you can't change a man who doesn't want to be changed. That which had waged, took years off my life. In trying to win his love, I compromised, which almost cost me my life. I was so close to being a statistic.

Now, I have a second chance. Involvement in an abusive relationship is out of the question for me. It's not worth it. A happy relationship is deserving of me, and I will not take anything less from this day forward.

Linda Foster currently lives in Pennsylvania. She is the parent of one son, Leon, and two daughters, Juakina and Mylisha. *Struggling For Love And Life* is her debut novel. She has also published poetry included in the International Library of Poetry, *Secret Hiding Places*. Linda Foster has written, as well as directed, several plays and skits. Her latest was, *The Judgment Line,* followed by, *Just in Time (part 2).* She has also been an extra in these movies: *Silence of the Lamb,* starring Jody Foster; *Warrior,* starring Tom Hardy and Nick Nolte; and *Three More Days,* starring Russell Crowe. Her training in Culinary Arts has led her to a devoted ministry of feeding the homeless and those in need. She is also the founder of "The Community Outreach Choir" which was birthed from the Soup Kitchen.

Have you ever struggled to make a relationship work? How far did you go? Were you hopeful that eventually everything would be all right? On the other hand, were you so much in love that you didn't care? Did it seem impossible to get out of the relationship once you realized your life was in danger?

This book is for men and women of all ages who have taken too many chances. Sarah Jones was one of those persons. She was looking for love in all the wrong places. Finding her Mr. Right was her ultimate goal. When she did, it was like love at first sight. Sarah tried to do everything she could for him. He was her knight in shining armor and no one could tell her differently.

In spite of the street life that her new man lived, Sarah was hopeful that his actions were temporary. She felt that by giving her all into the relationship, she would eventually win him over. Her efforts failed and her whole lifestyle changed in what seemed like a matter of moments. The mental and physical abuse took a toll on her. First, she struggled for love. Then she began struggling for her life.